GIRL WITH BLACK BAGS

By Juliet Grainger

Published in 2009 by YouWriteOn.com

Copyright © Text Juliet Grainger

First Edition

The author asserts the moral right under the Copyright, Designs and Patents Act 1988 to be identified as the author of this work.

All rights reserved. No part of this publication may be reproduced, stored in a retrieval system, or transmitted, in any form or by any means without the prior written consent of the author, nor be otherwise circulated in any form of binding or cover other than that in which it is published and without a similar condition being imposed on the subsequent purchaser.

Published by YouWriteOn.com

PRELUDE

Lucy jerked awake, her heart pounding in her chest. She lay there in the dark listening. A slant of light shone through the curtain. She listened again for her mother's breathing and rolled over, reaching out on the mattress. There was no-one there. Shivering, she crawled across the floor to the window, stood up, pulled the drape back and looked down. The street light outside shone onto the empty road lined with parked cars. "Mama," she whispered – "Mama." She was shivering with cold even though she wore her clothes. She knew it was night, but not the time. Bare-footed, arms stretched out, she made her way back to the mattress on the floor. She had pulled down the throw covering the window so she could let the light, dim from being three floors below, into the room. She crouched on the bed, an old army blanket pulled around her. She was so afraid. She was hungry – she had only had water and some soft, stale rice crispies to eat. The milk had been too sour to drink. The smell of rancid rubbish reached her nose and of stale beer from empty cans littering the floor. She listened again. She heard a car – was it her mother? But the car passed the flat and drove on. Then silence. Only the persistent tap dripping – drip – drip – drip. She counted until she reached fifty. The steady rhythm soothed her terror but her heart still raced. Where was Sarah? Had she been hurt? Was she in hospital? Or had she decided to go on her travels? Lucy buried her face into her knees and covered her head with the blanket. "Mama," she whispered. "Mama where are you? Please come home, I need you."

Chapter 1

The car stopped. Lucy sat in the front, a hard knot clenched tight in her stomach. She felt frozen, untouchable, it was a numbness through her body. 'Whatever', she silently said to herself. 'We are here dear,' said Janet, the woman accompanying her, in a bright and breezy voice, 'I know Veronica and Jim will be looking forward to seeing you.' The white door of the house flew open and Veronica and Jim streamed towards the car. 'Hello Lucy,' they smiled broadly. 'Lo,' muttered Lucy, her eyes cast down into her lap. 'Come in, come in both of you, Here Lucy, let me help you with your bags.' 'Bags,' thought Lucy contemptuously, 'bags' is the word. She looked at the black bin liners that acted as her suitcases being transported into the house. 'Old Bag,' she silently worded in her mind about Veronica. They unloaded the rest of the six black plastic bags from the boot, all bulging with the hastily packed contents of Lucy's eventful life. Veronica noticed that they smelt musty, and the faint whiff of cigarette smoke and cooking fat seemed to seep out of them. Already she was thinking what she could put in the washing machine to take the smell away.

They went straight into the kitchen. Janet thankfully accepted the offer of a coffee while Lucy had a fruit juice. She eyed it with disdain. She wanted a fizzy drink. The biscuits looked better. One sort was chocolate digestive and the other had jam fillings.

She nibbled a chocolate one and looked round the kitchen. It appeared big. 'I want another biscuit,' she said. 'Please,' hissed Janet. 'Oh don't worry dear,' Veronica smiled, 'Of course you can have another biscuit.' They then talked boring talk about forms, reviews and meetings while Lucy wandered round the room. Looking out of the window she saw the garden. Near the window was a tree with several bird feeders hanging on it and some greenfinches busily feeding there. It looked like a good friendly tree that you could climb. This was more interesting. 'Toilet,' she muttered. She thought this would give her a chance to see more of the house. She quickly put her third biscuit in her pocket and helped herself to another one. 'Through that door dear,' Veronica said. Lucy didn't like her sweet voice; it sounded so goody-goody. 'False old bag,' her inner voice said silently.

Meanwhile Jim had taken the bin bags upstairs. 'Would you like to come up and see your room, Lucy?' he called. This meant that she went up stairs followed by Janet and Veronica. It was a large white room. The curtains were blue and yellow, with a flower pattern on a white background, and she saw that the bed had her rabbit sitting on the pillow. Jim had spotted it on the top of a bag. Its grubby familiar grey body drooped, torn ear flopping, with one glass eye looking at her. She ran over and picked it up. She clutched it to her chest with feeling, nuzzling its soft ears. It was all right, she wasn't alone any more.

Chapter 2

Lucy had been at Veronica and Jim's home for a day. Her room was sorted. She now called Veronica Ronny. She liked it better. It was still the Easter holidays, but in a week she was due to start a new school. It was a village school in Batscombe in Somerset.

Lucy had never lived in a village with fields all around, containing sheep and black and white cows that she now knew were called Friesians, and that they originally came from the islands of the Netherlands. She loved collecting facts like these in her head. Most of her nine years had been spent with her mother in different flats in Yeovil and Bristol, and also in vans and old caravans. From time to time she had spent some weeks or months with different people, but a lot of them were now hazy in her mind. She'd spent the last ten days with a family after her mum drove off to Cornwall with her new boyfriend, leaving her at the social services office like a parcel. 'Take care luv,' she'd said, hugging her, 'We're having a bit of a holiday. You know how your mum needs it. Life's got really heavy. I'll be back before you know it!' 'Yeah,' Lucy had thought, clinging desperately to her mother, 'I'll believe it when I see you.' She knew her mother's promises. They were as reliable as the old rusty van, which was always breaking down. At least her mum, Sarah, had made sure she had Rabbit.

Lucy liked her bed. It was really comfy and warm and smelt fresh. The duvet matched the curtains, something she had never seen before. Often she'd been cold, with dirty old rugs and smelly coats for a cover. She knew Ronny was trying hard to make sure she felt at home. 'Fussy Old Bat' she now privately named her. She always seemed to be washing clothes and picking things up to tidy them away. She had insisted that Lucy put her things in drawers in her bedroom. She'd even stuck on labels as a guide. There were labels for pants, socks, tee shirts, jeans, and there were coat hangers in a walk-in wardrobe. Ronny had even shown her how to hang up her coat. 'Old Batty Bat,' she inwardly muttered. Secretly Lucy was relieved to have the guidelines because she had no idea how to sort her things. They had always been in piles on the floor, all mixed together. She found that calling people names secretly made her feel in charge. It stopped her feeling too sad. Being angry made her seem stronger.

One thing that Lucy really loved was her desk. The day after she had arrived, Jim and Ronny had taken her to a shop to choose it. It came packaged in a big flat kit, and Jim had built it with her in her bedroom. She had held the screws and he showed her how to drive one in with a screw-driver. The desk was made of a pale-coloured wood and it had a space on the left for her legs, and three deep drawers. Even better, they'd been shopping for things to put in the drawers. She now had plain paper, coloured paper and card, Sellotape, a glue-stick, scissors like at school and different coloured pens, with thick and thin felt tips.

She also had two scrapbooks and a photo album. Ronny had found some photos in her bags and explained that they were going to make an album of all the past and present experiences so that she would have something to remember. Lucy was appalled when she first saw Ronny touching the photos of her mother. A wave of rage had washed up inside her and she had grabbed the photos and the album from Veronica without thinking. She felt as if this woman was not only controlling her but taking the last piece of her mother away from her. Any changes felt as if she was losing the image of her mother that she had in her head. "Give em back to me, its me mum,' she had sobbed,' it's me mum, I don't want you touching her, she's mine!' Then she ran to the bed and threw herself into a kneeling position and pushed her face into the bedcovers crying loudly. Ronny had stood by helplessly, and when finally Lucy had raised her face she felt a small surge of satisfaction at the hurt on Ronny's face. Lucy wanted to hurt her. When she could see Ronny shocked out of her sorting and changing things, it made her feel better She was no longer a puppet. 'Old bag, old bag. Stupid old bag', she'd thought. Gradually Lucy had calmed down. She liked having all the things in her desk. She loved drawing and writing stories, so maybe things weren't all that bad. She thought of her mum and her eyes felt prickly. Did her Mum think of her, or did Dylan, her new man, make her forget? 'When she comes back it will all be different,' she told herself.

Chapter 3

Ronny had washed all her clothes. At first Lucy resisted bitterly. 'Cow, Cow, Cow,' she had wept. But after, when she smelt the clean fresh smell, she decided that it was a good idea. She had been afraid that the memories would be washed away, but they were all just as clear as before. Ronny had gently explained how the stale cigarette smell would taint everything else in her room, and the thought of this spoiling her bedroom had made her give in. Lucy hated her mum smoking those endless rollies and the yellow stained fingers and coughing that had kept her awake at night. Dyl had puffed away too. His nails had been black and his breath smelt. He used to pat her face and tweak her hair. She'd loathed it.

After a few days Ronny had asked if Rabbit would like a bath. Very reluctantly she had agreed. They went to a shop together where they had chosen special washing powder for delicate fabrics. Ronny had explained that this would keep Rabbit safe from damage. She even asked if she'd like Rabbit to have a new eye, but this Lucy emphatically refused. She did agree that Ronny could stitch up the torn ear so that it would last longer. Lucy had sucked them endlessly over the years which had done the damage. Rabbit was bathed. They did it together. After Rabbit was gently dried and repaired and aired in the linen cupboard he looked and smelt much better, and he was now a whitish colour. White Rabbit was now his name.

Ronny took Lucy to see the outside of her school. It looked all right. Unlike some of the big town schools she had been to it looked small. The playground was just a tarmacked courtyard, and there was a grassy part at the top shaded by some big beech trees. 'There is no meanness here.' Ronny said. 'The teachers and dinner ladies can see and hear all that goes on. 'Oh yeah,' thought Lucy, but she desperately hoped it might be true. She'd had so many cruel things said to her. The children in her old schools had taunted her. She had hated them.

She was taken to buy uniform. She even tried it on in the shop to see if it fitted correctly. No more second-hand leftovers of any size, often too big with chewed sleeves and stains. This time everything really fitted. Lucy had admired herself in the mirror. Navy skirt, pale blue polo and navy jumper. She had also got new shoes and white socks. The shoes were cool, she thought, real Clarkes and they were fitted by the shop assistant, both length and width, which was a new experience too. 'Gosh, I remember how Mum used to pinch shoes from shops and how they were sometimes too small and pinched my feet, and sometimes so big that they slopped and I kept tripping in them.' she had thought. She was too loyal to Sarah to say this out loud. She remembered the pain of the blisters and how often in winter she had had no socks.

Lucy also had her hair trimmed. She now had shoulder length brown hair. Ronny had got rid of the head lice straight away. She had refused to use chemicals and, using tea tree oil and conditioner, had patiently combed it through every day until every last nit was defeated. Lucy was really relieved not to be scratching and itching all the time. Her hair now looked shiny and well cared for. Ronny kept telling her what a pretty girl she was. 'Am I?' she thought, wistfully looking in the mirror. Her large brown, thick-lashed eyes gazed seriously back at her. She wanted so much to believe it, but she thought her thin body looked ugly. 'Still, I'm like the other children now,' she thought. When Ronny handed her some of the shopping plastic bags with the names of the shops printed on them, Lucy looked up from under her trimmed fringe and, looking Ronny in the face, smiled and said truthfully, 'Thank you'. This was the first time that she had said it and meant it.

Chapter 4

The first day at school was over. Lucy had been sick with nerves when she went that morning. This was harder than going to new foster homes. New adults were much easier than this. Lucy always had her mum with her in her thoughts. She was part of her. She used to dream how her mum was , and where they would live. Next time it would just be her and her mum. Dyl would have moved on and Mum wouldn't want a new man, only her. Only Lucy could make Sarah really happy. They'd get a flat and a dog and perhaps a cat if the dog didn't kill cats. Lucy would show her how to buy good food and how to put things away and keep it nice. She loved these dreams. They kept her being able to bear the fact that Mum wasn't like the other kids' mums. Lucy was going to make it all right.

Ronny seemed to understand that Lucy was scared about going to Batscombe School. Lucy had told her how the other children were mean and about some of the names she'd been called: 'Smellypants,' 'Nitbag,' Loopy Loo,' 'Looser,' 'Dirty.' The names seemed to be endless and they were engraved on her heart, It had been so hurtful.

Ronny had taken her over to a mirror. 'Lucy,' she had said firmly, 'Look at yourself in the mirror.' Reluctantly Lucy had raised her eyes up to the full length mirror. There she stood in her new uniform, her hair in plaits with two navy bands at the end of each. She did look good. 'Lucy, this is how the other children will see you. A very pretty girl in her school uniform, but there is something missing.' Lucy felt fear. 'What?' 'A friendly face. Show me a smile.' Lucy managed a stiff half-smile. 'Well, it's a start. Now tell me, what does a dog do when it's out for a walk, meets another dog, and wants to play?' 'Silly Old Bag,' Lucy thought defensively. Ronny persisted, 'Come on, Lucy, tell me.' 'Well, it wags its tail of course.' muttered Lucy. 'Exactly,' said Ronny. 'What happens if it puts its tail down?' Lucy thought for a moment. Ronny and Jim had a spaniel called Benjy and she was now used to going for walks across the fields with him. 'The other dogs don't like him; put up their hackles and growl.' She replied, beginning to catch on. 'There you are then, Lucy, you've got the answer to what's missing. Here you are, looking so lovely,' Ronny gave her a squeeze, 'the bit that's missing is from your face. Because you're afraid of what the children might say, you're going to school with your tail down, which is an unfriendly expression on your face. How can you wag your tail?…'. 'Smile?' asked Lucy. 'Exactly, you've got it. Mouth down and the children may growl. Mouth up in a friendly smile, looking interested in them, and they'll want to play. You'll be in a small class; only twenty with you, so they'll be delighted to have another girl to play with. Now it's up to you. Think of Benjy when he meets a new friend; his tail wags, he smiles.' Lucy thought about it. Yes, he did smile with his tongue lolling and eyes bright. Ronny went on, 'He bounces up to the other dog, they sniff, introduce themselves by smell and bounce around. Think about it.'

Lucy did think about it, a lot. When she was taken to school, Ronny came with her into the playground. A round-faced, friendly looking lady of about fifty came over to meet them, introducing herself as 'Mrs Boyle.' Lucy immediately imagined putting a boil on the end of Mrs Boyle's nose and on her rosy cheeks. 'Now she won't get the better of me,' she thought. 'Silly old hag.' The kindly lady smiled, seeming not to notice Lucy's hostility. 'Cally, can you come here and meet Lucy!' A small round girl came over. She had curly, long brown hair and pink cheeks. She beamed at Lucy. In spite of herself Lucy smiled back. 'I'm glad you're here,' said Cally, 'Do you want to sit with me?' 'Yes,' Lucy said, looking up from under her fringe, still smiling, 'Yes, yes I would like to.'

Chapter 5

Lucy, to her amazement, liked school. Batscombe really seemed to have friendly children in it. Lucy liked Cally. They shared the same table, and there were two other girls called Daisy and Amelia. The four of them played together at playtime. They were really interested in Lucy's imaginative ideas and seemed to admire her. The first day two boys had tested her. Sam flicked pencil shaving at her from the next desk. He was a tall dark haired boy who was used to being looked up to. He was stunned when Lucy stood up and retorted, 'Hey, green-snot boy, what do you think yer doing?' Sam blushed, and Ben next to him said in his defence, 'Sam did nothink.' 'Oh yes he did, Wax Ears,' Lucy stormed, 'and if you do it again I'll 'ave you.'

Then Mrs Boyle quickly intervened and the children all went back to work. Lucy muttered under her breath, 'Boils, Boils, Boils, Boils (Beastly Boils),' but the class recognised it was not a good idea to mess with Lucy and there were no more attempts to tease her. Mrs Boyle, who knew all about Lucy's past, didn't make an issue of it and the episode was soon put into the background. In the cloakroom Sam offered Lucy a sweet.

When Ronny came at 3.15 to collect her, Lucy walked out quite serenely. She called out 'Bye' to friends and joined Ronny. She handed her her bookbag just as if she was her mum. She liked being seen with Ronny because it made her feel like the others. She wasn't going to let on to Ronny though. She hoped her mum wouldn't mind. She felt a bit guilty. One of the things she noticed that Ronny had done was to come to the school early. So often her mum had been late, and sometimes not even turned up at all, but Ronny was always there. It took away that butterfly feeling in her stomach, the one she always got at the end of school which came from fear that she might be the only one left behind.

Chapter 6

After Lucy had been with her family for three months, Janet, her social worker, arranged to pick her up from school and take her out to Macdonalds. Janet had explained that it was to be a treat for her, but Lucy knew better. She knew that Janet wanted to question her to see what she thought about her family. She knew too that what she said would make all the difference as to whether she stayed or moved on to another family. She knew that the power was hers. Lucy had had two postcards from her mum in Cornwall. They just told her that Mum and Dyl were still travelling. No address, and no stamps on the cards. Lucy reckoned that they had been nicked. The first had a picture of St. Ives with people surfing, and the other one said, 'The bay at St Agnes.' Mum had written they had dolphins there. Lucy was thrilled. She had always loved dolphins. The night after the card arrived she lay snug in her bed, the duvet right up to her nose. Her bed was her safe place where she could dream and wish. That night she imagined her mum, without Dyl, turning up in her large van to take her away. 'Lucy,' her mum had beamed,' you and me are off to Cornwall! Quick get Rabbit, we're going to live on a beach, surf, eat chips and milkshakes everyday, and swim with the dolphins, just you and me forever.' Lucy had fallen blissfully to sleep, and in the morning it was hard going to school, knowing that her mum wasn't going to collect her.

Janet, her social worker, waited for her at the school gate. She wore a long brown skirt, ankle boots with high heels, made of some sort of fabric material and a weird cotton hat decorated with a mauve crocheted flower. The brim was turned down so you could hardly see her eyes. The hat was brown too. 'Batty Hatty,' thought Lucy. Janet greeted her in her deep actressy voice. 'Lucy dear, you do look cool in your uniform.' 'Not weird like you,' thought Lucy. 'Lo,' she said. She'd told her school friend Cally that an old aunt from Australia was taking her out. Luckily none of the other children seemed to notice she wasn't with Ronny, or that the woman she was with didn't have an Australian accent.

At Macdonalds Lucy ordered a chicken burger and chips with a large milkshake. Janet had a black coffee and chattered on about school, and asked her all about her work and the books she was reading. Lucy was able to tell her she was doing well. Everyday Ronny and Jim had supported her with her homework. Ronny had really helped her with her handwriting, teaching her with a special book how to join up her letters properly. Fascinated, Lucy had practised diligently and now her work was really neat. Ronny had also taught her how to keep her work well presented and how to cross out neatly, now that she was writing in pen, and how to use the rubber on her special biro. Twice she had work displayed at school and she'd been awarded three gold apples for excellence. She really was like the others now!

As she'd expected, Janet started the investigation: 'And how is it with Ronny and Jim, dear?' 'Here we go, Batty Hatty,' she thought. She looked up from under her neat fringe, fingering the band on one plait. 'Oh fine thanks.' 'How are you getting on with your foster parents?' Lucy felt a rising heat in her chest. She hated that 'foster' word. 'They're not my foster parents. They are the people I live with. They never call me a foster child. They say I am part of their family, that I live with them. I'm not a foster child.' 'But Lucy, I think the word 'fostering' is really nice. Sort of warm and friendly.' 'Well I don't!' stormed Lucy, really upset now. 'I hate the word, hate it, hate it. Nobody else has a 'foster' mum. I'm part of Ronny and Jim's family – I am, I am!'

Janet obviously thought it was time to change the subject. She pursed her lips and tried to look understanding. 'Stupid cow, weirdo, cow, cow, cow!' thought Lucy. She suddenly thought Janet might take her away. She blurted out, 'I like Ronny, I like Jim, I like Benjy, I like the house, I like school and Cally and Daisy. I want to stay. I'm going to get a hamster for my birthday if I want. Ronny said she'd teach me to clean it and feed it. It will be all mine, and I feed Benjy sometimes and I take him for walks.'
Janet was satisfied. Lucy certainly wasn't holding back on information.
'How strange,' mused Janet, 'that she doesn't like being called a foster child, how strange!'

Chapter 7

It was July 21st, Lucy's tenth birthday. Lucy had woken up early. As soon as she was awake, Ronny and Jim had come in to sing her Happy Birthday. They were carrying a pile of presents, and they had made her a card. It was a photo of her with Benjy in a frame. There was a big parcel wrapped in brown paper, with lots of perforated holes in it. 'My hamster,' screamed Lucy, ecstatic. She fell on it, gently tearing away the paper. The hamster was out of its bed. It was tiny and golden, with a white patch on its body. 'Oh,' Lucy breathed, 'it's a baby, Oh.' She was transfixed. 'I'm afraid, Lucy, you can't take it out yet,' explained Ronny. 'She's new, a baby, and nervous. She has to get used to her cage, and all the new smells, and learn to recognise your voice, and then very gradually you can lay your hand in the sawdust, so she can get to know your smell, then you can start to handle her.' 'I want to call her "Jessie,"' whispered Lucy. She was really happy. Unable to help herself, she went to Ronny and hugged her – and did the same thing to Jim. I've never had anything I wanted more. Then she opened her other presents. She had three books, a really nice recorder, and a first practice book of music. 'You can use the music stand in the study,' said Jim.

There were several cards; one from Ronny's parents and one from Jim's mother, one from Janet, one from Mave, a previous foster carer, and even one from Mrs Boyle, her teacher. There was one more card from Ron and Jim. In it was a piece of paper telling her that she was going to start jazz ballet classes on a Wednesday afternoon. Cally and Daisy were doing them. 'Oh, just like the others,' she gasped. She rushed her breakfast and ran to the front door. 'I'm waiting for Mum's card,' she said. She waited, and at last the post came. A card from Cally, a card from Daisy, but no card from Mum. Tears filled her eyes. She felt as if she couldn't swallow and the heavy feeling that had left her came back. 'Mum has forgotten me,' she thought. 'Oh no, Mum has posted my card and present late,' she said in a hard tight voice.

Chapter 8

It was Saturday. The day of her party. Lucy had asked nine friends. It was the time that the Moscow State Circus was coming to Yeovil. Ronny and Jim had managed to get twelve half price tickets. They chose the matinee. They had arranged for the parents to drop all the children off, and they were going to get the bus back to Batscombe at five o'clock. The circus was magic. Lucy was spellbound. She was dressed in jeans and a new pink top, with a new denim jacket. She felt really good. Her hair was washed loose and shiny, and her cheeks pink with excitement. Ronny had packed a bag of snacks and drinks for everyone. Lucy felt proud. She was doing everything that the other children did, and they were all glad to be with her. Lucy loved it all, especially the trapeze artists. 'That's what I want to do,' she thought. 'How my mum would love this.' She thought again. 'But perhaps she would have been drunk, or out of it. Maybe she wouldn't have liked it and anyway I couldn't have brought my friends.'

It was just before half time and the clowns were coming back in. The ringmaster walked grandly into the ring. 'I want to announce the birthday of a little girl called Lucy Griggs who is ten! Where are you Lucy?' Lucy looked at Jim and Ronny, who smiled and nodded. She put her hand up.
'Can you come out here Lucy? We would like your help.' Aghast, Lucy stepped out of her seat. Cally gave her a little push. The two clowns came forward

and Becko helped her over the low wall into the ring. 'Lucy,' said Maxo, the sad looking clown, 'Can you pull this rope, and I'll help you?' The rope went out of sight, out of the ring to behind the entrance curtain. Lucy pulled, and pulled, and pulled, and pulled, and more and more rope came into the ring. She had to pull quite hard. Suddenly she fell back and Maxo caught her. On the end of the rope was a tiny Yorkshire Terrier, trotting happily across the ring. Becko picked him up, and the crowd clapped and whistled their approval. Lucy was lifted back over the wall and made her way, crimson cheeked, back to Ronny and Jim. 'How did you do it?' Lucy asked, in the interval. 'We went especially to the circus yesterday to ask,' said Jim, 'as I had the morning off for a meeting.' 'Oh,' said Lucy. She couldn't think of anything else to say. It was too amazing.

Chapter 8

At last a letter arrived from her mum. The paper was pink with a matching envelope. Lucy tried to imagine which shop her mum had nicked it from. 'Smiths,' I bet.' There was no mention of her birthday. It was a letter full of complaints. No one was giving her and Dyl a flat. She was expected to go to court. Of course she'd been nicking food, how else could they eat? It went on and on. Lucy cried at the end. This wasn't how it was meant to be. Where was her mum? Did this mean she wasn't coming for her? Court probably meant prison, and prison meant she'd have to visit her mum in there. She hated prisons. She had visited her mum in them before. They felt horrible, and the visiting rooms always had a horrible smell.

Ronny found Lucy crying. She saw the letter. She didn't say anything; just held out her arms and Lucy sobbed onto her shoulder. Recently, she had felt a real need for Ronny's hugs. They were warm and comforting, and the tight little feeling of loneliness disappeared. 'Oh Lucy,' said Ronny, 'I know its hard, and I know you're disappointed, of course you are. Sometimes life if full of disappointments. Its like winter. You think the sun will never shine again, and the garden looks so unkempt, brown and dreary, but the sun always does shine again and all the bulbs come up again, in spite of winter, and suddenly the garden is full of Spring and colour and hope. Life is full of joy again. It will be like it for you. It seems very dark now, but joy will come again. You'll see.'

Lucy felt comforted, and safe and warm. With Ronny around she was ok. 'Now Lucy what do you want for tea? Don't forget Jessie needs cleaning out today. I'll give you a hand.'

Chapter 10

It was now six months since Lucy had arrived at Beech House. She was loving her school. For the first time in her life she had made friends. Ronny and Jim had spent a great deal of time helping her with her work and social skills. Every evening and at weekends she had learned to sit down for meals at a long square oak table. At first this had been really hard. She had despised Ron and Jim for their insistence. They had introduced all sorts of drippy ideas such as napkins, water, salads and lots of vegetables. She had really kicked hard at the vegetables, and the five portions of veg and fruit a day idea, but they paid no attention to her complaints. The minging old drags, as she silently called them, just calmly explained that these were their house rules, along with an ordered bedroom and desk. In their household these rules were as important as Benjy's daily walks, and in feeding and cleaning out Jessie. After a few visits to her friend's houses, Lucy began to realise that their parents were doing the same sorts of things. They too fussed about salads and vegetables and fruit. The first time that Ronny put a roast dinner in front of her, Lucy had protested with a real tantrum. 'I don't like it, I won't eat this stuff, you can't make me. I'll tell my mum on you, I will, I will!' Ronny appeared not to notice. She just calmly removed the plate and put it back in the cooling oven. She and Jim tucked into their dinner, while Lucy watched mutinously. 'I want to go,' Lucy muttered. 'No, Lucy,' said Jim firmly, 'This is

Sunday lunch, and this is when we eat.' The chicken was followed by strawberry ice-cream and home made meringues. 'Give me that,' Lucy demanded, 'I want that now!' 'No Lucy,' Ronny patiently answered, 'we don't have seconds without at least trying our first course.' 'It's not fair, it's not fair,' snivelled Lucy. She felt really hungry now. 'Look, Lucy, this is how it is, try some of your dinner, and you can have pudding afterwards,' said Ronny, 'and that's all I'm going to say.' So finally Lucy backed down.' I want my dinner,' she said through gritted teeth. She hated losing face. Without a word, Ronny brought her dinner from the oven. She put it in front of Lucy. Lucy tried it, and to her surprise it tasted really good. 'It's bearable,' she muttered.

Chapter 11

Lucy was dreaming. She twisted and turned in her bed, wet with perspiration. It was the same dream she had had before. She was wandering in a sort of wilderness. The grass was overgrown and there were two rusty old burnt out cars, as well as ugly junk. She could see a disintegrating mattress with its insides falling out and a rusty brown bedstead. There was a damaged fridge dumped down a slope and old pieces of wood from rotting furniture. She was all alone. Her bare feet were freezing, the ground felt squelchy and cold and mud oozed in between her toes. 'Mama, Mama, Mama!' she cried frantically, 'Mama, Mama, where are you?' but her voice was the only sound she could hear, no one was there. 'Mama, Mama!' she was beside herself now. She felt so frightened, so alone, 'Where are you? – Mama, Mama!' Nobody came, Lucy began to run still crying out. She was sobbing and her sobs sounded really loud in the silence. There was an eerie pale dawn light, making everything silver. She was desperate. She screamed again, 'Mama, Mama, where are you?' She felt as if she was the only person alive in this cruel, cold world. 'Mama!'

And then a gentle voice broke into her dream. 'Lucy, Lucy its all right, it's Ronny, its Ronny. I'm here, you're safe, you're safe.' She felt a warm hand stroke her damp hair away from her brow. Lucy came back gently into her bedroom. She realised it was only a dream. Here she was in her own bed. Ronny sat down on the bed, and Lucy put her head on her shoulder. The dream still felt so real, so terrifying. She clung on to Ronny, and huge sobs wrecked her. She felt Ronny's arm around her. 'I thought I was all alone, I thought I'd never find Mum, I thought I'd be alone always – that I'd have to be on my own in that horrible place.' Ronny said nothing; just tightened her arm round her shoulder and continued to smooth her hair off her face. 'It's a horrible place, all cold, and horrible old things are there. It's a place of rubbish – everything is rotting.' Lucy started to cry louder, 'I'm so scared, I'm so scared, I want Mum, where is Mum, why won't she come? ' Lucy's whole body shook with sobs, with desolate anguish, with fear and grief. This world was so scary. She pulled away from Ronny, and in spite of herself, she kicked her legs and thrashed her arms. It felt too awful this feeling. So painful. Ronny sat quietly beside her. Every so often she said softly, 'Lucy, I'm here, you're quite safe, just let yourself cry – its all right, you are so safe here.' And Lucy writhed and cried and struggled with that pain and loss, and after a few minutes she could cry no more. She lay back on her pillows, silent sobs still shaking her body as she clutched Rabbit to her. Again Ronny stroked her fringe back off her face. It felt so good, so comforting. 'I've got a headache,' she said, her voice croaking from the harsh crying. 'I'm sure you do, darling,' said Ronny. 'One second, I'm just getting you a cold flannel,' and she slipped out of the room to the linen cupboard, got a flannel, wetted it and brought it back to place on Lucy's forehead. 'You'll feel strange, but it's a really good thing to express that pain – really healthy,' said Ron. Her eyes were kind and reassuring. Lucy lay there looking up into them. 'You see,' said Ronny, 'all those fears and hurts are kept tight inside you. They all get stored up. Well, you know the pressure cooker I use in the kitchen?' Lucy nodded weakly. 'Well it's like that. All that hurt and pain is like steam building up, and with the pressure cooker we have to let that steam out from time to time. That empties out some of the pain, and later, when your headache is better, you'll feel very tired, but much calmer inside.'

Jim came into the room. He was carrying three cups of warm hot chocolate, which was Lucy's favourite, and three digestive biscuits. 'Here you are my darling,' he said, sitting at the end of the bed. 'Ronny will plump up your pillow and you can sit up for your chocolate, then I'm going to read you this Tony Ross book, 'Reckless Ruby.' It's one of your favourites, isn't it?' And, even though it was three o'clock in the morning, he did, and they all drank hot chocolate and nibbled biscuits. Lucy didn't feel afraid anymore!

Chapter 12

It was late August and Ronny, Jim and Lucy were going on holiday for a week. They had a room in a small hotel in a place called Looe in Cornwall. Lucy had longed to see Cornwall. She knew her mum and Dyl were around there somewhere. If she couldn't go on holiday with her mum it would be the next best thing being there with Ron and Jim.
Their bedroom was lovely. It had a big double bed in it, and Lucy saw with delight a TV. It had a big chest of drawers and a wardrobe and even a machine for pressing trousers. 'I'll show you how it works.'
There was an annexe to this room, with two beds in it. 'This is your room.' Lucy smiled. Ronny, seeing her excitement said, 'Lets put Rabbit on the pillow. You're right nearby us, if you have any dreams.' Lucy had her own bedside table with a light over the bed. She put her book on it. She was reading 'Pollyanna'. She liked the 'glad game,' which was about thinking of all the good positive things that were happening each day. She and Ron and Jim were going to try playing the game while on holiday.

She also had her own cupboard and chest of drawers, and her own basin. There was also a little attached bathroom off Ron and Jim's room, for all of them to share, with a bath and shower. 'What a lot of things I've learnt about,' she thought. There had been lots of times in Lucy's young life when there had been no washing at all. She had had to be taught really obvious things by Ronny – like how to use the loo,

wipe her bottom correctly, and how to wash using soap and rinse, as well as how to wash her hair. Lucy learned very quickly. Her desire to be like her friends was a real incentive. She didn't want anyone to notice she was different.
'Shall I help you unpack?' Ronny asked. 'No thanks, I'll do it myself.' Lucy couldn't wait to make her own little house in her room. She put her carefully folded summer clothes into the drawers. She decided to put her swimming things in with her underclothes in one of the top drawers. She hung up her two dresses. One was a sun dress of pink checks. Lucy loved it. She had pink canvas shoes to match. The other dress was white. It had embroidered flowers on one of the two pockets. It had been made in India and came from a shop called Tradecraft. They had bought it in a town called Glastonbury, on a day out. It was the sort of dress her mum would have liked. Sarah, her mother always wore long flowing skirts and indiany type scarves and long dangly earrings. Her mum was really pretty. She was very thin. She usually had bare feet in the summer and her legs and arms were brown. She had long brown hair in dreadlocks. 'Your eyes are like mine,' she'd sometimes told Lucy. Her mum had lovely long fingers, although she bit her nails. Lucy loved her laugh. It was deep and husky. 'Probably because of smoking the rollies,' thought Lucy.
Lucy laid her folded clothes lovingly. They were hers, all hers. They weren't from a jumble sale. They weren't nicked from a charity shop. They had been bought especially for her. Even her shoes were specially fitted to her feet and chosen for the way

they looked. 'When I was begging,' she thought, 'I always wanted beautiful clothes like the other children I saw, and now I have.'

Chapter 13

'This is like being in heaven,' thought Lucy. She couldn't get over the wonder of being by the sea. Everyday brought new and wonderful experiences. In the harbour there was a big black one -eyed seal that came in with the fishing boats. 'Does he bite?' she asked a fisherman. 'He certainly would if you touched him,' the fisherman said. He was old and burnt a mahogany brown by years of sun and wind. His face reminded her of a cliff-side, all pitted with crags and crevices. When he smiled she saw he had his two front teeth missing. 'Perhaps he's a secret pirate,' she thought, 'smuggling rum and whisky.' They had been to the Smuggler's Museum at Polperro, and she was now an expert on pirates, smugglers and shipwrecks. 'Leave 'im be, and 'ell leave you be,' said the fisherman. Then to Ronny and Jim he said, 'You've got a bright girl there.' 'Yes,' they both said, but Lucy noticed that neither said she wasn't theirs. 'They aren't ashamed of me,' she thought with a rush of pleasure.
Each day was an adventure. Boat trips round Looe Island, and more at Falmouth and St. Justins. They rowed up the Looe Estuary, where Jim pointed out Egrets, which had been really rare until a few years back.
One blue skyed, blue sea day they spotted common dolphins near Falmouth, from their boat trip. Lucy was thrilled. She couldn't wait to tell Sarah.
Everywhere they went Lucy scanned everybody, searching for her mum. She had this dream that her

mum's old van would arrive at the place wherever they were. Her mum would see her and shriek, 'Lucy, Lucy!' and run towards her, with her arms held out. 'Lucy,' she would say, 'Oh Lucy, I'm never going to be apart from you again, I've been so miserable without you!' Dyl would be there in the background but a long way back. In fact, his only purpose would be to fetch and carry for her and her mum, like a taxi man. Sometimes this daydream was so powerful that she would come back to the real Cornwall, minus her mum, with such disappointment that she would snap at Jim and Ronny and be really cussed and mean. One afternoon they had arranged a special boat trip along the coast to look for seals and dolphins. Lucy had been shown how to pilot the boat and had been able to have a go herself, but instead of showing pleasure and thanking them at the end, she told them that it was a rubbish trip and really boring. Jim and Ronny's faces looked really hurt. This gave her a strange satisfaction because it helped to assuage some of her own pain that she felt in not finding her mum.

Later that day Jim took her aside. 'Lucy, you are really moody. We've gone to a lot of trouble to give you a lovely holiday. When you're the bright friendly girl we've come to know, we really enjoy ourselves, but when you're tough and moody, it's no fun for us at all. It makes us want to go home.' 'Tough,' muttered Lucy. 'Look, Lucy, you wanted us to go to the rock pools with our nets this afternoon. Well, this afternoon, the answer is 'no!' 'Until you have a pleasanter mood all crab catching and rock pool searching is off the agenda. Instead, you can come for a walk along the cliffs.'

So that is what they did that day, with Lucy sulkily dragging her feet far behind them, but in spite of her determination to spoil their walk, she began to forget herself because she was too busy scanning the blue green sea below for dolphins. By tea time Lucy was back to being cheerful she couldn't wait to tell Cally and Daisy all about her holiday.

Chapter 14

'Why did you want me?' she asked Ron and Jim one day at supper time.

'Well, there are many reasons,' said Jim. 'As you know, we have a son, Nick, who has finished university and is having a gap year in Africa working for an Aid Programme. He's twenty-two now.' 'Yes but why me?' Lucy insisted. 'I think we've always longed for a little girl in our life,' said Ronny. She looked really serious, and Lucy found herself looking at her closely, as if for the first time. She saw a woman in her forties. She had dark honey-coloured hair, which was cut short but waved around her kind face. Lucy saw she had deep laughter-lines round her blue eyes. Her mouth was wide, and she had a dimple on the left side. She wore very little make-up, just a bit of navy mascara and pink lipstick. She smelt nice, an earthy, warmish, baking smell. She often wore a rose scent. 'In fact,' thought Lucy, 'the whole house has this special baking smell. You're much older than my mum,' she thought, 'at least forty something. My mum is beautiful like an angel.' Then she quickly thought, guiltily: 'But a very grubby angel.'

Ronny then continued. 'Three years before Nick was born I had another baby, a little girl, but sadly she died at birth. Ever since, we've always wanted a little girl.'

'Why did she die?' said Lucy. 'What did you do?' 'Nothing,' said Jim hastily. 'Just occasionally, something can go wrong with a pregnancy.' 'It's very rare,' added Ronny, 'very unusual, but this was one of those sad things. Its very unusual,' she added again, as if afraid that Lucy would think lots of babies died. 'I know,' said Lucy, 'I know all about it, my mum had two dead babies. It's called miscarriages you know. But my mum's doctor told her it was the stuff she was taking, and the drinking. He told her she was lucky even to get pregnant with all the stuff she was taking. Did you do that too?'

'No, no, no!' said Ronny, looking horrified. 'In fact I was really careful all through the pregnancy. I ate well and didn't drink any alcohol, but just something went wrong. I was very, very sad, and I cried a lot like you do when you're sad.' 'Oh,' said Lucy. 'Anyway that was twenty five years ago. A very long time ago, and then we had Nick and we were very happy.' 'Why didn't you have another baby – another girl then?' said Lucy. 'We wanted to Lucy, we really wanted to, but although we wanted another baby, we never had one. We even had tests, but we never discovered the reason why. But then when Nick went to university at Exeter, we decided we'd do a training with social services, so we could look after a little girl.' 'Oh,' said Lucy. 'And was I like you thought I'd be?' 'Yes I think you were' answered Jim,' We never thought we'd get a girl who was so pretty and intelligent though.' 'Do you really think I am? You're making that up,' Lucy said disbelievingly 'No, we're not,' they both chorused together.

Lucy turned her attention to Jim. It was funny; she'd never really seen either of them. Suddenly they seemed to be people with real feelings. They'd both felt sad. He was old too. Probably older than Ronny. He was tall. About six foot. They'd been doing measuring at school. He wore old brown corduroy trousers, and a big baggy grey-green jumper. He wore heavy brown shoes. He had a slightly ruddy face. It's from always being in the garden thought Lucy. He loved gardening. Lucy had given him the affectionate nickname of "the old sod", but he was somehow earthy and comforting and cuddly and safe. He worked as a garden designer. 'In fact they are both gardeny,' she thought. Ronny had been a part time nurse, while Nick was growing up, but when their son left home she did a floristry course at the local college, and now she worked with a friend, doing flowers for weddings and parties. She also helped out in the local flower shop when their staff were ill. This meant that there were always flowers around the house. Each week she put some in Lucy's bedroom in a tiny white vase. Lucy loved this.

'Now you have me, do you wish you had someone else?' Lucy continued.
'No,' they both said unanimously 'We think you're amazing. You are really unique, Lucy,' said Ronny. 'Every child is unique, every child is special, and to us you are very special and very loveable.' 'Well, most of the time! Let's be realistic here,' twinkled Jim. 'But even when you're quite hard-going, we still think you're ok, even though your behaviour could be better.' Lucy grinned. She really liked their

truthfulness. It made her believe in them. 'I've got to go and feed Jessie now' she said, and stood up to go.

Chapter 15

During the summer holidays Janet arrived again to take her out to Macdonalds. She wore a summer version of her long winter skirt in a thinner material, and pointy shoes with a sling-back, in beige. She had a straw hat on still, with the brim pointing down. She wore long sleeves, and lots of rings on each hand. 'D'you know where my mum is?' were Lucy's first words. When Janet said 'No,' Lucy was surprised that she wasn't too disappointed. It meant she could stay with Ron and Jim. She'd got quite used to it now, and she didn't want to change schools. 'Oh she'll be in touch when she's had enough of dolphins and rock pools.' said Lucy airily. She knew today's outing with Janet was preparation for the six-monthly Social Services review meeting, and that Janet wanted to fill out her form in preparation for it. Lucy decided she would be at this meeting. No one was going to make any decisions without her being there.

A week later Ronny took Lucy to the Social Services building for the meeting. Jim was at work so he couldn't come too. 'I'll be thinking of you,' he said, as he kissed them goodbye that morning. They entered a small hall, painted in green, with some plastic chairs. Opposite was a sliding glass window with a hatch that opened into an office. On the wall were grim posters. Lucy read each one: 'Child Line…' Then there was one saying, 'Have you been abused? Do you need help? Ring…' 'Is there violence in your home? Tel…' 'Confidential: The

AIDS helpline is…' Another poster said, 'Do you have a problem with alcohol or drugs? Ring…' 'I wonder if Mum and Dyl have seen that one,' thought Lucy.

She looked curiously at the hatch. It slid open and a book was shoved towards Ronny. 'Can you sign yourself in please,' said the voice from the other side. Ronny did so obligingly, and the secretary pressed a button that released the door so Ronny and Lucy could go through. 'God,' said Lucy, 'this is just like a prison. Who do they think we are – muggers?'

They followed the Secretary through to another room lined with chairs like the ones in the hallway. The walls were painted pale green. The chairs were beige. A jug of very orange squash was on the table and a plate of biscuits. 'Chocolate ones,' thought Lucy. Janet was there, still in her hat with another long skirt with flowers on. 'Would you like tea or coffee?' she said to Ron. 'Tea, please,' 'Biscuit?' she said, first handing the plate to Ronny and then to Lucy, who took two. Janet handed her a mug of squash. There were two other people there. One slim, efficient-looking lady with a neat bob, who had a notepad and biro on her lap, and another Social Worker lady. She had short red hair, and green nail varnish with long manicured nails. She wore clog-like slip-ons. The sort that were meant to be good for your feet. Lucy gave them all names. 'Sugary Janet,' 'Slithery Secretary' and 'Slimy Social Worker.' She looked at them from under her fringe, defiantly. She couldn't help chewing her biscuit with her mouth open and lolling back in her chair. 'That will upset Ronny,' she thought. 'I told her I hated these meetings.' Slimy Social Worker started. 'What white skin you have,' thought Lucy spitefully. 'You match your green nails.' 'Now, how is everything going?' she said to Ronny. 'Well we are very happy with everything,' she answered. Lucy was aware that Ronny hated this event as much as she did.

'Now, Lucy, how are you getting on with your foster parents?' The word 'foster' was like a red rag to a bull for Lucy. She sat up and glared before retorting, 'Don't use that word. I hate that word. Why won't you listen?' She turned to Janet. 'I told you, I am not a foster child. I am Lucy, I am a person called Lucy who lives with Ronny and Jim. I have a mum, and I live with Ronny here, I am not a foster child. I hate that word – do you hear?' Her rage made speech pour out of her. Lucy by now was quite red in the face. 'I hate these meetings. I like Ronny and Jim, I will stay with them as long as I want to and then my mum and me will make other plans. She and me will decide. I hate you all, I hate you all!'

There was a silence, a very awkward silence. Lucy felt scared and she put her hand into Ronny's without realising she was doing it, which was silently noted by the three women. 'More coffee, tea, anyone?' said Slimy Social Worker. The Slippery Secretary was writing busily. Janet said, 'Well, Lucy and I had our little talk and I think the next six months will be fine.' Slippery Social Worker nodded. It seemed Lucy was staying where she was. They then mumbled about new targets all being much the same and Slithery Secretary scribbled some more. 'Well that's all for this review,' said the red haired lady. Lucy and Ronny left and went out to a Chinese restaurant for a special lunch.

'Well Lucy,' she said smiling, 'I think you made yourself very clear. I certainly heard you, but don't you think you could have been a little kinder to the Social Workers? They only want your happiness. 'Do they?' Lucy smiled. 'I'm hungry. All this has given me a really big appetite. Can I have crispy seaweed and sweet and sour chicken?' No one is going to muck up my life again she thought.

Chapter 16

Lucy was very excited. Cally was coming to her for the day and for a sleepover. Lucy wanted it to be perfect. It made her feel that she was just like the others. She knew that Ronny and Jim would give her support and she wouldn't have to feel ashamed. Cally was going to sleep on a camp bed in her bedroom, and it was all prepared. Ronny made it up with a duvet and Cally helped get the pillow cases on. She tidied her room specially and even picked some roses to put on the windowsill in Cally's honour. At school she had checked on her friends favourite food. It was pizza. 'I'll tell you what,' Ronny said, 'I'll get the ingredients, and perhaps you and Cally would like to make your own pizza? I'll be there to help you, and we can make a chocolate cake at the same time. I think you'll find Cally will enjoy doing that. It'll be something different.' 'I hope so,' thought a worried Lucy.

The day arrived and the weather was beautiful. Ronny showed both girls how to cook the pizza and they also made and washed a salad together. The food smelt really good, and both girls felt really proud of their efforts. Although it was a margharita pizza, they made it with mozzarella cheese, tomatoes and added pineapple, ham and olives. It was a real success, and whilst they ate it, they had a chocolate cake in the oven all ready to be iced with butter icing when it had cooked and cooled. They also blended yoghurt and strawberries for a dessert. They were really pleased. 'I've never cooked like this before,' said Cally, 'I love it.' Lucy felt really glad inside. Now she would want to come again.

The whole day was a success. In the afternoon, when it was slightly cooler, Ronny and Jim took them both for a walk with Benjy. They walked along the river. It was an area where otters had been seen regularly, and Jim explained to the girls how to look for otter spraint. He told them all about it, and Lucy shared her knowledge of how to look for it, and how to look out for signs of water voles, and to look at the grass by the edge of the river to see if it had been gnawed. Jim often took her on wildlife watches along the river. Benjy dashed ahead, his stumpy spaniel tail wagging. His nose permanently fixed to the ground as he followed the scents of animals in zig-zag patterns. He was a creature of habit, and at various spots along the river he would dash down the bank to stand up to his chin in the water to cool himself, his long black ears floating on the top of the water. Then, to screams of protest from the girls, he would come out and briskly shake himself all over them.

They didn't see an otter, but they did see some spraint on a rock. Jim showed them the threads of white which were fishbones. He let the girls sniff at it. It smelt of hay. He explained that if it had been mink it would have stunk of fish. Cally was really excited. Jim showed her some grasses that had been nibbled, the tops cut flat across, and pointed out two vole holes in the opposite bank. There was no sign of any voles. Benjy had put a stop to that, but they did see a kingfisher streaking down the river, and caught the flash of turquoise as it passed again shortly afterwards, flying back up the river, giving them a second sight, even clearer than the first. They saw three mallard ducks, two drakes with one female, and two swans with their five grey cygnets. Then, just to make the afternoon perfect, they saw a female roe deer on the edge of the woods across the valley. Cally told them that she'd never known about nature before, even though she lived in a village. 'I do think Jim is cool. Fancy him knowing so much. I wish my dad did that.' Lucy was exultant. In the evening, they watched an old video together of Matilda, and had a late snack together. Then, curled up in their beds, they chatted. It was late when they finally fell contentedly to sleep.

Chapter 17

'How am I going to explain that I am living with you?' Lucy had said to Jim and Ronny. It came out of the blue shortly after she had arrived in their home. Ronny and Jim had turned to look at her. They were sitting at the table having lunch. They gave her their undivided attention. 'What do you think you'd like to say Lucy?' Jim had said, 'Have you got any ideas?' Lucy chewed the top of her thumb nervously. 'Shall I tell them my mum runs off and does travelling?' She watched them thinking. Jim took a piece of french bread and spread butter on it. Then after a bite, he fixed his gaze on her again. 'Perhaps, Lucy, we could word it slightly differently. You know you don't have to give any details. You could say something like this: Mum is travelling, so Ronny and Jim asked me to live with them. Or you could tell them she isn't too well, so you live with us. What do you think?' Lucy thought long and hard. She knew it was important to get this right. She knew only too well that if she told all the truth she would be teased, and the other children would ignore her. She had experienced it all before, and the memory of the pain made her feel quite sick. She wanted it so badly to be different this time.

'I think,' she said, her grey eyes looking at them for approval, 'I think we could say she's – what's the word? – recouping.' 'Convalescing,' Ronny suggested. 'Yes, I think I might say she's convalescing after being ill, and travelling, and you were friends and I asked to live with you.' 'And how we were really keen on having you,' added Ronny. 'What do you think?' Lucy chewed her thumb-top anxiously and looked at her plate. 'That sounds very sound to me,' said Jim. 'What'll I say about it when she comes back?' asked Lucy. She was looking up now. 'Just say it hasn't been decided,' Ronny said. 'How does that sound to you?' 'I like it,' Lucy replied, relief all over her face. 'Right-o, that's decided,' Jim said smiling. 'Tell you what, lets have a practice. We'll be the children at school, asking you questions, and you can have a go at answering.' And for the next ten minutes this is what they did, until Lucy felt confident. Really confident.

Chapter 18

A few weeks later a phone call came for Lucy. It was Janet. 'Lucy dear, how are you?' 'Fine,' mumbled Lucy. 'Look dear, I've had news from your mother. She'd like to see you.' Lucy felt a lurch of unexpected fear in her stomach. 'Is she coming to get me?' Suddenly she was really afraid of being taken away into another chaotic unknown situation. She had dreamed so many times of it happening, but now it felt a real possibility she was scared. 'No dear,' Janet said reassuringly down the phone, 'I'd like to come and see you and explain. I will take you down to Cornwall, to a place called Truro, and we will be in a special room and your mum will see you there. Then I'll bring you back to Veronica and Jim's house.' 'OK,' Lucy said in a tight little voice, revealing none of her feelings. 'I'll come tomorrow after school then, I've had a word with your fost...' Janet broke off, remembering this was not what Lucy wanted to hear. She carefully rephrased it, 'Veronica and Jim are quite happy to see me tomorrow. I'll be there about four.'

Lucy put down the receiver and, overcome with confusion, burst into tears.
Ronny, seeing Lucy's reddened face when she came into the kitchen, dropped the flowers she was arranging for a silver wedding party, and gave her a big hug. As she had talked to Janet before Lucy, she knew about the proposed visit. She sat with Lucy, who had started to sob again, keeping her arm around

her until she had quietened. 'Do you want to tell me what has upset you, Lucy? I know it's about the visit, but do you want to share it with me, what is hurting?' Lucy tried to explain. 'You see I always dream of seeing my mum, and being back with my mum, and how it all will be different – but,' she started to cry again, 'but when I thought it was all over here and I'd be going back, I felt really scared – and then there's school, and my friends and…' Lucy started to cry louder.

Ronny waited quietly while Lucy sobbed onto her shoulder. Ronny gave her a tissue. Somehow Ronny always had a spare supply of tissues. 'Those nice soft ones,' thought Lucy, 'the ones with stuff in them for red noses. They smelt nice.' 'What are you most afraid of Lucy?' prompted Ronny. 'Of being cold and hungry and lonely and never knowing when mum is coming back, and of her injecting herself, and of being drunk, and of her getting into trouble and ...' Lucy lent her face on the table, her arms under her face, and shook with anguish. All those horrible memories were coming up and it hurt. Hurt. After a moment she wiped her face with her sleeve, carried away by the memory. 'I don't want to feel like that, I don't want to be dirty, I hated being cold, and I don't want to have to steal food. I don't want to eat only chocolate bars, and pot noodles, I just don't want to be like that again - I don't.' By now Lucy was indignant and fierce.' I had to wash in puddles, I had no warm clothes. I was cold and hated being alone at night and trying to sleep at night and people tramping in and out. I hated it, I hated it. My shoes were all holey.' Her anger spent, she looked at Ronny, afraid she had said too much. 'It wasn't my mum's fault,' she said loyally, 'she was ill then, she'll be better now, she promised me she'll get her head sorted.' Ronny stroked her hair back from her hot face. She felt feverish. 'It's all right Lucy, of course you feel these things. You had some bad times, and of course you love your mum, she's your Mum. Nobody's going to make you do anything you don't want to do. You are safe.' 'You can't live with your mother now; not until she's better and can look after you properly. You see you are very important, and all children have to be kept safe and properly fed and warm, and above all safe. You are going to be kept safe, and we love looking after you. Now if you're going to visit her, we'll have to think of some nice present you can take her. Let's think of some ideas.' Lucy smiled weakly, she liked that idea. 'What about making something with baking dough?' suggested Ronny. Lucy felt safer. It was as if the pain was being taken off her shoulders. It was such a relief. 'My mums going to get her head sorted,' she whispered to herself.

Chapter 19

It was the school play. They were doing the musical, "Honk" and Lucy had the part of a pig in the farmyard. She was part of the chorus, and was going to sing a verse with Cally and Daisy who were also pigs. Lucy loved practising. Ronny was really keen on doing drama. She had taught Lucy how to say her lines with real expression. She taught her things about diction, and how to breathe properly. She'd told her that next term she could have some singing lessons at school because she had a lovely, tuneful voice. Lucy loved this idea. She loved being on the stage. When she was acting she could be anybody that she wanted. They'd made paper mache masks at school and hers looked very pig-like. It stopped just above her mouth so it didn't block out any sound when she was singing.

Ronny was not any good at sewing, so her own mum, who Lucy called Nan, came to stay for the weekend, and on Saturday she and Lucy went into town to buy some pink material from which she made three costumes for Lucy, Cally and Daisy. They both came to be fitted. Lucy felt important. She got on really well with Nan, who was just like a granny. She was tubby, with grey hair, cut in a wavy bob, Her blue eyes were nice and crinkly, and she laughed a lot, a gargly, belly laugh. Lucy had called her Crinkly Wrinkly in her head. She told Lucy stories about Ronny as a little girl. She'd been quite naughty, she explained. 'Always getting into scrapes.' 'Did you hate her when she was naughty?' said Lucy, curiously. 'Of course not, smiled Nan. 'There are always times when you don't like a certain behaviour, but you still love that person. Sometimes another person annoys you, and you need to have space and walk away for a bit, but you soon feel better and want to be with them again.' 'My mum often said she hated me, especially when she was on the booze,' said Lucy. 'Maybe,' answered Nan, 'but it certainly didn't mean she meant it. She might have been all upset and cross at the time, but that feeling wouldn't have lasted. I know she loved you.' 'How?' said Lucy. 'Because she's your mum, and you are her beautiful little girl. You were her baby. It wouldn't be possible not to love you, Lucy. And I'll tell you something else,' said Nan, her blue eyes twinkling, 'When people are angry, its much more to do with themselves than with the other person. You see Lucy. People make a choice. They can choose to be angry, or they can choose not to be. If they can't control their anger, it's their problem.' Lucy was really surprised. She wanted to think about it. It was something very new to her. 'When people are naughty at school, the teacher doesn't scream and explode.' Lucy said. 'Exactly!' said Nan, 'She's made a choice.

The first evening of "Honk' had arrived. The dress rehearsal had been the day before. Several things had gone wrong, but Mrs Boyle and Mrs Weston, the two teachers running it, had been pleased. 'Poor dress rehearsals mean good performances,' they said. Lucy had felt sick with excitement and nerves. She was sweating in her pig costume and her hands felt clammy. Her face under the mask felt hot. She knew Ronny, Jim, Nan and Grandad and Janet were all there watching. 'I wish my mum was here,' she thought. 'My mum being good' she thought. 'Not Mum being embarrassing.'

The curtain rose. She watched Honk, the duck, from the side. She loved the way Jason, the boy playing the part, did swimming strokes across the pond. He sang very well. Then it was her turn. As she came onto the stage with all the animals, dressed in their different animal costumes, her nerves seemed to fall away. She found herself really enjoying it. She remembered all the words and sang loudly. She, Daisy and Cally sang their verse really tunefully. It was great! The applause at the end was really loud and she knew that her family and Janet would be clapping her especially.
  'I like my life.' Lucy thought, as she walked forward in a line for the encore. 'I like my life!'

Chapter 20

Janet and Lucy had been driving for three hours. They had stopped outside Exeter for a baguette lunch. Lucy scarcely tasted her cheese and tomato one. Usually it was her favourite, but today it felt as if something was stuck in her throat. She hardly touched her Appletizer. The car heater was on, and Lucy was wrapped up in her pink hooded coat, but her fingers still felt like ice. It was November, and everything outside looked drippy, and grey. 'Like I feel,' thought Lucy. She had longed for such a long time to see her mum, but now it was really happening, she was afraid. 'Please Mum, please be changed. Please be nice. Please let it be better.' But she didn't know what to expect. On the back seat were two models she had made out of play dough and carefully painted. One was of a doll, made to look like Lucy, with brown curly hair. Lucy had been really proud of the hair. She had pushed dough through the garlic press in the way Ron had taught her, and it looked brilliant. She painted the face with rosy cheeks and a happy smile, 'Like me,' she thought. 'This is how I look now.' She had painted her in a denim dress, and given her navy shoes like her favourite school Clarke's ones. The other model was of a dog with long spaniel ears like Benjy. She painted it in Benjy's colours: black ears and a black-and-tan body. Its head was a bit big for its body, she had thought critically, but she liked it. She had picked a posy of herbs. There was lavender, the flowers no longer blue, and rosemary and two very late November yellow rosebuds that had never opened. Lucy and Jim had planted the lavender and rosemary bushes in the garden, nearly a year ago when she'd arrived, to remember her mum by. He had dug the hole and she had watered the plants in their pots, taken them out, put them in the hole, after being shown by Jim how to tease out the roots, and then watered them in, after filling in the holes with compost, and then stepping on the soil to make it firm, in her new green boots. She thought back to all that time ago. She had thought it a daft idea. She remembered how she called Jim 'the Silly Old Sod,' because he was always out in the garden in his large wellies, brown cord trousers and baggy old jumper. 'Silly Old Sod, always playing about in the mud.' But Jim had been right with his idea, she now thought. She loved picking her own lavender and rosemary for her bedroom, and in the summer, every time she'd smelt it she had thought of her mum. That way she was all somehow associated with the nice smell, and she'd imagined her mum smelling of sea air and wild herbs from down there in Cornwall.

They were now crossing the Tamar Bridge at Plymouth. All through the journey Janet had tried to make conversation, but Lucy had stayed obstinately silent. She felt very tight inside. All locked up. She couldn't get out of that feeling. It was like being locked in a fortress, and the key which would enable her to come out was missing.
Then she saw it, a sign saying Cornwall. There was no turning back. 'Maybe,' she thought, 'Mum won't turn up. It wouldn't be the first time.' Then she felt

panic. What if she didn't? How did she even know if her mum was alive? She hadn't had a postcard for two months.

Lucy looked out at the bare trees and the brown fields. Even the few sheep and cows she'd seen looked dispirited. How different this Cornwall looked. So unlike the green lush blue-skyed place she came to with Ron and Jim when they had stayed in Looe. At last the almost empty dual carriageways turned into busier traffic and it seemed like no time at all before she saw Truro on a big sign, with a picture of a cathedral on the same board. Janet had to park, and took out a map to see where she was going. They only had to ask once before they drove into a car park. She saw a small sign saying Social Services, and a sign saying Family Pl– There was no time to see the next word. They'd pulled into a marked space. Lucy got out of the car slowly and opened the back door to get her carefully wrapped presents. They were in pink paper, and she'd stuck some butterfly stickers on them. She picked up her posy, and a brown paper bag. Ronny had made a picnic for her and her mum. It had cheese sandwiches, her mums favourite, and four chocolate penguin biscuits, with two apples and two small cartons of orange juice. Lucy felt uncomfortable. Would her mum make fun of the presents?   They were led into a room, after going through a procedure when they had to sign their names before the locked doors operated by codes could be opened by a lady sitting behind a glass window in front of them. It made Lucy feel she was going into a prison. The room was painted blue this time, and had sea pictures of Cornwall on the walls. This time the plastic chairs were of pale blue. The carpet was chocolate brown. Lucy reckoned it was to hide the dirt. There was a table in the middle with four chairs round it. She saw cigarette burns on it and an old grey ashtray. The room had a stale, unwashed smell of old cigarettes. 'It smells of unhappiness,' Lucy thought. Where was her mum? Wasn't she coming? She and Janet sat in silence. Lucy looked out of the window at the dripping trees, and a bare muddy lawn. In the corner of the room was a plastic marble-run without any marbles and some old metal toy cars, and a box with pieces of Lego in it. There were also some battered-looking books for children. It seemed like hours, but was in reality only two minutes before the door opened and her mum was escorted in. 'Lucy baby!' she cried, and opened her arms. Lucy leapt off her chair and rushed over to her. After a bear hug her mum held her away and looked at her. 'Oh Loo, how you've grown! You look…you look different. Have they been treating you well? You tell me if they haven't. I'll have something to say about it, you'll see.' Lucy nodded, and they sat down. Janet left the room.

'Oh Lucy, I have missed you. Have you missed me?' Lucy nodded. 'Have they been good to you?' she said again. 'I bet it's not like with your old Mum,' she went on. Lucy answered truthfully 'No.' This time out loud.
'We did have a laugh didn't we, you and me?' Lucy nodded again. 'We will again, you'll see, it won't be

long. Me and Dyl, we've got plans, you see, we'll get a nice little place of our own by the sea, Luce, and a dog. You see if we don't.' Lucy nodded again. This was familiar talk, she had heard it before. It hadn't always been with Dyl, it had been with other men too; all a bit misty in Lucy's memory. But they had all been similar.
'Oh Lucy, you and me are going to have such fun, you and me. We're going to have such fun.' She stopped and took out a plastic pouch. Her 'rollies,' and her papers. 'I'll just roll a fag, Lucy. All this has made me nervous.' She placed the orange strands of tobacco in the middle of the paper, expertly smoothing them along before rolling a smooth, narrow cylinder and running it along her tongue to seal it. Lucy couldn't help noticing her yellow stained fingers as she watched this familiar ritual. She had forgotten it. They had been learning about smoking and all the harm it did to the body at school, in PSHE. Mum's lungs must be filled with tar, like in the film she had seen.

'Lucy, life's been a real bummer, it's not fair. Did I tell you, we haven't been given a flat, we're still in the van. I got hauled up again, and I have to go to court. It wasn't my fault, Lucy, honest, you know how it is.' Lucy nodded miserably. 'Life's so unfair. You know I've got to get money, well, they won't give me the money we have to have, and, it's hard down here, so me and Dyl, we decided it would be a laugh to nick a few things from a shop. We had it all planned too, but they caught us, and I ran out, only the van wouldn't start. And now they're making such a fuss. I told them it wasn't serious, only a laugh, but they're treating us like major criminals. I told them my doctor said I need to be on a programme, but you know how it is.' Lucy bowed her head again in agreement. She did know how it was. She looked at her mum with a frown on her face. Did her mum really not know how she was fooling herself? Or did she really believe this self-deluding? Lucy really didn't know the answer. But she could see clearly her mum hadn't changed. It was she who had changed.

Chapter 21

Lucy and her mum spent the next two hours together. They shared the picnic. Her mum liked the flowers. Lucy wished she'd shown more enthusiasm about the presents, but she also understood that her mum would be jealous of Ronny and Jim, and she'd prepared herself for this in her mind. When her mum questioned her about them she answered very cautiously, and tried to sound unenthusiastic. She was really sincere about her school and her friends and her mum was pleased for her. She had hated Lucy being unhappy at school.

Sarah looked critically at her daughter. 'My, you do look posh.' she remarked, 'Not like my little free spirit.' Lucy said nothing – 'And you talk posh too' – she fingered Lucy's denim jeans and blue jumper. 'Look at this, all posh and new!' She rolled herself another cigarette, and then started to tell Lucy again all about her problems. Lucy listened patiently and sympathetically. Sometimes she thought, 'you are the child, and I am the parent. It's all the wrong way round.' Then Sarah suddenly shrieked, 'Lulu, what've you done to your hair? Where's your dreadlocks?' Lucy's face went red. 'They were cut 'cos of the lice,' she whispered.

Chapter 22

Janet and Lucy drove back to Batscombe slowly. 'What car is this?' Lucy asked. It felt friendly and safe and the seats smelt of leather. Janet explained that it was an old car called a Morris Minor – specially done up. It was basic, but Lucy loved it. Janet did too. It had a character. The car even had a name: Jezebel. Janet had called her that because occasionally in the winter the car had refused to start and let her down, making her late for work. Lucy liked the idea of a car having a name. It made it into a personality.

They stopped in Devon at a pub. Now they were on the way back Lucy suddenly felt hungry. She was glad to have seen Sarah and to see that she was well and all right, but she was also surprised to find herself feeling glad to be going back to Ronny and Jim's. She realised that she had been afraid that her mum would ruin it all and insist that she went back with her. Now this clearly wasn't happening, Lucy realised that going back felt as if she was coming home. It was a new feeling, this feeling of belonging somewhere, and of knowing what her life was all about. In this past year she had made friends and she had learned to trust Ronny and Jim. She knew they wanted the best for her and that they were really there for her. They supported her in every way, even though they nagged and had rules. Lucy thought about her bedroom and her warm bed with real affection. She couldn't wait to get home and snuggle up in her bed.

Janet talked to her over the fish and chips they were eating . It was really cosy there, and to their great delight there was a crackling log fire to sit by. Lucy wrinkled her nose. She loved the smell of a wood fire

and the throat-catching smoke rising from it. It reminded her of fires she had played round when she was little, and of the bonfires that Jim had made in the garden that autumn, after carefully checking under the wood to make sure no hedgehogs had slipped beneath the leaves and branches to hibernate.
'You know, Lucy,' Janet said, 'Sometimes I think you feel I'm your enemy. You know I only want what is best for you. I am fond of you. I really care about your happiness, and I am here to protect you. I had to remove you from your mother because at the time she wasn't able to care for you.' Lucy looked up from her plate. 'I know,' she said.
'You see, social workers are here to make sure that you are properly cared for in all ways, and that you are kept safe.' Lucy nodded wisely. 'Lucy, are you angry with me for taking you away from your mum? Are you very sad to be going back to Batscombe?' Janet felt pleased with herself that she hadn't said the words 'foster carer.'

Lucy munched on her chips while she pondered. And then it all tumbled out in a stream of words: 'I don't hate you, I understand you are my care- worker. I know it's your job and its all right I'm not with my mum. Sometimes I'm sad but I like my school. I like being with Ron and Jim. I like being like the other children with a family, but can't you see? It's really hard having a social worker 'cos it makes me weird. The others don't have social workers round their necks do they? I mean, if they knew I had a social worker, they wouldn't want to be friends with me. I hate Mum always being under Social Services, it's like being a stray dog in a dogs home. They have dog walkers. I know 'cos Ronny took me there to see the dogs. I don't want to be a dog in kennels with a walker and people feeling sorry for me, thinking I'm dangerous and that I bite or something. I want to be normal like the other children – I want to be a dog in a home, not a cage, I want to be normal!' 'But Lucy,' Janet began. 'No, let me finish,' spluttered Lucy. 'You asked me. Can't you see every time you use that word 'fostered', or 'looked after,' you remind me and everyone else that I am not the same as everyone else, that I'm different. I hate being different!' Tears welled up in Lucy's eyes and she turned away. 'But Lucy dear,' said Janet gently. 'Lots of children are fostered. There's nothing wrong with being fostered. You know, there is a drama group in your area for lots of children who are in care.' Janet carefully left out the word 'foster.' 'Also, this Christmas, there is the party for you all, and there's the summer barbecue. I'm sure if you met some of the others, you wouldn't feel different.'

'Can't you see it would! I don't want to be different like them, I want to be me, like Cally and Daisy with a home and with people like them. I hate the word 'in care' too. I hate the whole thing. Why can't you see? It's not my fault Mum's like she is. She's all right,' she added loyally. 'It's just I want to be just the same as everyone else.' 'I see,' said Janet gently. 'And don't tell me I'm *not* like the others!' almost screamed Lucy, '"cos I *am*, and I *am* going to be normal. Ron and Jim don't make me feel different. I'm not different. I even go for sleepovers and my friends want me back at their houses. 'Of course, Lucy,' reassured Janet. 'Of course they do. Now, would you like some ice-cream? They've got some lovely ones on the menu.' In spite of herself Lucy looked at the list. They had. 'I'll have the butterscotch one,' she said.

Chapter 23

It was Sunday, the day after the trip to Cornwall. Lucy felt weird when she woke up, even though the sun was streaming through the curtains. She couldn't explain how she felt – just angry and tight inside.

'Are you all right Lucy?' asked Ron, as Lucy morosely ate her cornflakes. 'Mmmm.' 'Sure?' said Ron. 'You don't look to good.' 'Of course I'm sure, can't you leave me alone!' And at that she pushed back her chair and stormed upstairs, shutting her door with a bang. Ronny was halfway out of her chair when Jim said firmly, 'Leave her, Ronny, she's all churned up by her visit to Sarah.' 'But…' 'No buts, Ron. Let her cool down. If you go up now it'll only get worse. Let her have the space to sort her feelings out.' Ronny felt hurt, but she could see Jim's point. Meanwhile, upstairs, Lucy sat on her bed, and for no apparent reason she put her head down on her pillow and cried. She didn't feel sad. She felt angry and she wanted to hurt somebody. She gripped her pillow hard. She didn't understand why she felt so rotten. 'I hate you,' she said, 'I hate this world, I hate everybody, I hate everything.' She cried even more heartily into her pillow. Then, aware of her snotty nose, she got up for a tissue.

Her eyes fell on Jessie's cage. 'I don't hate you, Jess,' she muttered guiltily. Then she sat on her bed, and stared at a poster on the wall. It was a picture of a bay Arab horse, galloping across a plain. 'I don't hate you,' she said. Gradually her temper died down. Lucy thought about her mum. 'Why do you have to be different?' she thought. 'Why can't you change and love me like other mums love their children? Then my life wouldn't be like this.' She tried going into her favourite day-dream of her mum and she getting a flat together, and how it would be. But the dream just wouldn't work properly because she just couldn't see her mum changing into this new kind of mum. Lucy suddenly felt incredibly tired and sad, and she just lay down and looked at the ceiling. Lots of memories drifted through her mind. Her mum playing with her and lifting her high in the air. 'Lucy Babe, you and me do have fun don't we?' And Lucy saw herself as a little girl of four or five beaming, her long dreadlocks falling over her eyes. Then she saw her mum shouting: 'Get out Lucy! Leave me alone! I'm having a fix, and I don't need no kid messing my head up!' She saw herself trying to sleep in some long-forgotten flat, under old blankets that smelt mildewy and of grease and unwashed bodies. There were loads of people in the room, and music was blaring. She couldn't sleep, she felt so tired and afraid of all the noise. Some people sounded angry. Their voices were very loud and someone smashed a bottle against a wall. In one corner some people were huddled over something. They were sniffing and they were laughing. 'Mum, Mum,' Lucy had whispered, but she couldn't see her. Then she saw herself in the van. She was cold and alone. 'I'll be back soon, Little Rabbit,' her mum had said, but it wasn't soon, her mum had been out all night. She was scared and crying and very, very hungry. After even more hours her mum was back with a strange boyfriend. 'Look, Luce,' she said, 'I've brought you some crisps and chocky biscuits.' She threw them to Lucy, and then she and the man had gone straight to sleep. Lucy ate what she had ravenously, then went outside to play by herself. She'd felt ok now her mum was back.

Lucy came back into her room and realised where she was. She hated these memories. They hurt her. They hurt where her heart was. A real, physical pain. It was like having a piece of glass stuck in there. 'Perhaps I have a broken heart,' she thought. Then, feeling hollow and lonely, she went downstairs where Jim and Ron gave her a big hug and explained to her that her funny mood was quite normal. 'I don't hate you.' Lucy tried to explain, 'It's just that….' Then she burst into tears.

Chapter 24

Sassie the cat was getting fat and lazy. She'd stopped going out so much, and spent a lot of time sprawled on Lucy's bed. She luckily took no interest in Jessie. She seemed to understand that the hamster was not something she was allowed to eat. Lucy loved Sassie being on her bed. It made her feel special and liked. 'I think she likes me best,' she said to Jim one day. 'I think she does,' grinned Jim. 'She's just like you, she knows her own mind. She used to sleep on Nick's bed, but since he's left home, she's really glad to have a new friend. Lucy felt a small spark of anger when she thought of Nick. Although she hadn't met him yet, she felt jealous that Ron and Jim had him. She wanted them to love her as much as him, but she reckoned that they couldn't, because she wasn't theirs, and he had been with them as a baby too.

After a few weeks Ronny was stroking Sassie. 'You know Lucy, I think Sassie is pregnant.' Lucy came over. 'Here, put your hand here.' Lucy did. Feel how hard her sides are said Ron. They did feel hard, not squashy like on a fat cat. 'Look Lucy, if you keep your hand here, softly like this, I think you'll feel a movement.' Sure enough, there was a faint movement under her fingers. Lucy's eyes widened and she exclaimed, 'Oh!' in real wonder. 'Well, Sassie, you fooled me,' said Ronny, smiling, 'and how many surprise kittens are you going to give us?' For the next two weeks Sassie had special food, and nobody chucked her off the bed. She just made short journeys outside and then came back to sleep. Ronny and Lucy lined a cardboard box with newspaper and put it beside her bed. 'She likes your room so much Lucy, I think that's where she'll have her kittens. She feels safe with you.' Lucy smiled proudly. Each day the cat was gently lifted into her box. Sometimes she settled there for a few minutes, but very soon after she'd be back on Lucy's bed. Each night Lucy went to sleep with her near the bottom of the bed. One particular night Sassie was restless. She kept jumping off the bed, and then jumping back again. After a while Lucy fell asleep. About five in the morning Lucy was woken. She heard a loud purring. Stretching her feet she felt something damp under the duvet at the bottom of the bed. Sassie was making little mewing sounds and then a loud crooning purr. Switching on the light Lucy cautiously pulled back the duvet. There was Sassie, purring in a way Lucy had never heard before. Then tucked under her brown nose Lucy saw a tiny damp black head. It had closed eyes, and a pink nose, and tiny flattened ears. 'Oh!' she breathed in amazement, 'Oh, Sassie!' Then, realising what was happening, she ran across the landing to Ron and Jim's room. She burst in, forgetting to knock in her excitement. 'Jim, Ron, wake up, wake up. Sassie's had a kitten!' Both of them were instantly awake, and soon all three of them, huddled hastily in dressing gowns, were back at Sassie's side. This time there were two kittens. This second one, larger that the first was ginger. Sassie crooned, purred and licked them almost ferociously. 'Look how proud she is, Lucy,' whispered Ronny. Sassie seemed pleased they were there. She seemed to be saying, 'Look what I've done, aren't I clever.' Then she mewed again and stretched out. And from under her tail emerged a third kitten, black, tan and white. It was all wet and sticky with a membrane over it. Immediately Sassie turned to lick it clean. The kitten moved under her rough tongue. 'Look, Lucy, they're all alive. Oh Sassie, you clever girl,' said Ronny, stroking her head. Sassie's yellowy green eyes were bright and wide. Then she went back to her washing. 'Well, we'll leave her in peace. Maybe there will be another one.' But the tortoiseshell was the last kitten. When they went back in twenty minutes Sassie was lying on her side, making little chirruping noises. The kittens had wriggled enough to be against her still-fat tummy. They were nuzzling her sides, looking for teats. The ginger one had managed to find one. 'He's the strong one,' said Jim. He'll probably be the biggest.' Gently, Ronny picked up the black one and placed its little nose against a pink nipple, then she did the same for the tortoiseshell. After a lot of bumping and nuzzling their little pink mouths fastened on, and Lucy watched entranced. As they sucked their tiny front paws pushed against Sassie's side, and Sassie opened and closed her eyes as if in a trance of contentment. 'Oh,' said Lucy, tears of wonder in her eyes. 'It's just like magic.' 'Just as well you have a mattress cover, Lucy,' said Ronny. 'We'll leave them to get to know each other for a couple of hours. Then we'll put them all in their box.' Lucy smiled. She didn't mind one bit that Sassie had chosen her bed to have her family.

Chapter 25

When Lucy first arrived to live with the Carpenters she thought Ronny was quite strange. She knew that she had a room at the top of the house that was totally hers. 'It's my sanctuary,' she told Lucy one day, 'my own private space.' The room was alone, at the top of the house, up five steps. 'Please don't go up there, Lucy, not without my permission,' Ronny had said firmly. 'It will be more that you life's worth, Lucy, to go up there,' laughed Jim. This made Lucy start imagining all sorts of things. She talked to Cally about it. 'Perhaps she's a witch,' said Cally hopefully.' I've never met a real live witch. Or maybe she does weird experiments or something up there.' Lucy looked carefully at Ronny the next time she saw her. She didn't look like a witch, with her thick hair tied back off her face. She usually wore blue jeans, shirts and fleeces, and looked countryish, as if she rode horses not broomsticks, Lucy remembered that Ron had grown up with horses and that she did love riding.

One day, when Cally came to tea and Ronny was clearing up the kitchen after their spaghetti, Lucy and Cally decided they would go and look at the room for themselves. So, leaving Ronny occupied in the kitchen, they went upstairs to Lucy's bedroom, and then very quietly up the little flight beyond. They tiptoed up and talked in hushed voices. The white door with a round brass handle was firmly closed. Very gingerly Lucy turned the handle. It swung open soundlessly. They both listened nervously for sounds from below. They could hear faint clattering from the kitchen below. Cally turned on the torch they had brought with them from her house and flashed it round the room. In front of the window was a desk with a laptop on it. In the opposite corner was a shelf with lots of candles and a pile of brightly coloured cushions on the floor beside it. The carpet was of beige matting that Lucy knew as sisal. They had it in the study downstairs. On another wall was a white bookcase filled with books – all sorts, and lots of paperbacks too. 'Look, said Cally, 'they're thrillers. I recognise some of them. My mum reads those too.' By now Lucy was feeling nervous. 'I think we'd better go down.' So, slowly and quietly, they closed the door and crept down the wooden stairs. As they reached the bottom the landing light came on and there was Ronny. 'Oh, there you are,' she said, seeing their two flushed faces, 'I was just coming to ask what time Cally's mother was expecting her'. 'Lucy,' she said firmly, 'what have you been doing? You are looking so guilty. Have you been up in my room?' Lucy blushed red and hung her head. 'So, girls, you've discovered my secret, have you?' Ronny looked amused rather than cross. 'What do you mean?' asked Lucy. 'My secret life,' said Ronny.

Seeing the alarm on the girls faces, she smiled. 'No, seriously, it's not as bad or as sinister as you think, it's just the part of my life that's just for me.' You see, I'm a writer. I write articles and stories. I'm writing a travel book now. It's the part of my life that

I keep separate. 'What are the cushions and candles for?' said Cally bravely. 'They're another part of my life,' Ronny replied. ' I do yoga, so I keep mats up there, and the candles and cushions are for meditation. Sometimes friends come and do it with me on Wednesday mornings, when you are at school Lucy. It's something I love to do, and that room is my place of peace and creativity.' Lucy was surprised. 'I never thought you did that. I thought you only did flowers. 'Well, that's it exactly, Lucy. We've all got lots of sides to us. I love my job and looking after you of course, but I also have hobbies that feed me too like my writing and yoga. They are my relaxation. You know I go to a writer's circle once a month.' Lucy nodded miserably. She felt that Ronny was getting too like her own mother with the yoga and meditation. She hoped that this wouldn't come in the way of Ronny not having enough time for her. Cally however, looked very impressed. On the way home she said 'Cool Lucy, your mum is very wise isn't she, and clever.' Lucy wasn't so sure. She thought Ronny was really embarrassing. She hated her standing out and being different.

Chapter 26

It was three weeks to Christmas. This was to be Lucy's second Christmas and she was excited. The first Christmas had been a bit of a blur for her. Everything had been so new and strange. She had never had a proper traditional Christmas with her mother and all the rituals of buying and decorating the tree, wrapping presents, writing a letter to Santa and putting up decorations had seemed almost dream-like. This year was different, she knew what to expect, and she found herself looking forward to choosing the tree and searching for presents. She loved buying the wrapping paper, and making labels with Ronny out of last years cards. She liked making the gingerbread men biscuits, and she made homemade fudge for Jim with Ron's help. She bought Cally and Daisy a pair of rainbow coloured gloves that would stretch to any size. She bought Ronny a large notebook with a hardback shiny cover in pink for her writing, and Jim some packets of seeds including carrots, sunflowers and nasturtiums. She bought her mum a woolly hat with ear flaps, a scarf and gloves. They came from a Peruvian shop. She bought Dylan a leather wrist band from the same shop. She chose her cards with care. She bought one pack showing children from around the world, and the other had a picture of a robin. Because they had a robin daily in the garden which Lucy loved to watch, she liked the idea of having a pack of robin cards, set in a snowy scene.

Lucy had one anxiety, which she kept tight inside her. She knew that Nick, Ron and Jim's son, was coming on leave from Africa for three weeks, and she dreaded it. She knew how much his parents were looking forward to seeing him. She clenched her hands together and chewed the inside of her bottom lip as she thought about it. She had a tight hard feeling in her tummy. 'I hate him,' she whispered to herself, 'I hate him, I know he's going to be horrid. Oh why does he have to come and spoil everything.' She brushed away a hot angry tear. 'I was just getting used to the place and felt I belonged here, and now he's coming and it will all be ruined.' She could imagine it all so clearly. She saw Nick's smiling face as it looked in the photo on the piano. He'd walk in and everyone would rush to him and love him and there'd be nothing left for her. She'd be invisible. The more Lucy pictured this, the more she could see herself as an inconspicuous grey little mouse. 'An orphan mouse,' she thought, 'that nobody wants, and with nobody to stop the cat from eating her'. She kicked the fireplace. It hurt her toe. 'All right, Lucy? You seemed a bit bothered,' called out Jim from his armchair. 'I'm fine,' lied Lucy. 'I think I'll take Benjy for a walk.' 'Good idea,' agreed Jim. He knew she was hurting. He reckoned that a good windy walk would be just what she needed to blow the bad thoughts away. 'When you get back,' he smiled, 'we'll have crumpets for tea'. 'Great,' said Lucy, listlessly.

Chapter 27

It was the day of Nick's arrival and Lucy, Jim and Ronny were waiting at the arrivals barrier at Heathrow Airport. It was Lucy's first trip to the airport, and she held tightly to Jim's hand. She was afraid of getting lost in the throng of people. Ever since she'd been small, she'd had this terror. Her mother always seemed to be striding ahead of her on fast legs and Lucy had never dared to take her eyes off her in case she disappeared. Her own short legs were always running to keep her in sight. This had left Lucy feeling very vulnerable in any new place. The feeling that she'd be left behind and alone remained strong, and she was grateful for Jim's warm reassuring hand in hers. He seemed to understand her fears even though she was unable to express them. Jim and Ron behaved in the opposite way to her mother, they were always keeping an eye on her to make sure they couldn't lose her.

Lucy couldn't help sneaking quick peaks at their faces as they waited at the barrier. She could feel their excitement and eagerness to see Nick. Lucy's stomach felt knotted and very angry. She recognised that she was jealous. 'Why doesn't anybody feel this way about me?' She thought back over some of the times she'd seen her mum after being separated. Her mum made all the right noises, but after a very short time she always appeared indifferent to Lucy. She loved to have her daughter as an audience, but she never wanted to hear much about Lucy herself. It had taken Lucy quite a time to understand this and notice it. The truth of it really hurt and a wave of pain flowed over her. It was a real physical pain in her heart, and it made it difficult for her to breathe properly.She felt light headed.

Suddenly people started to flow through the barrier, and all at once there was Nick, tall, tanned and long legged like Jim. He was beaming as he came towards them. He hugged Ronny hard. She only came up to his shoulder and then embraced Jim, and they both slapped each other on the back. Then, hugs over, he turned and looked for Lucy. 'Hi,' he said, 'Hi, Lucy, its really good to meet you.' He held out a large, slim hand to shake hers. 'I've really been looking forward to meeting you.' His smile and face looked so genuinely friendly that Lucy couldn't help giving a tight smile back. He was already melting some of the rage and fear that she held inside her. 'Let's go and get a coffee, Ronny suggested.' 'Good idea,' Nick agreed, and as they walked towards a café he put his arm loosely around Lucy's shoulders. 'I'm really looking forward to hearing all about you. Do you like croissants, or are you going to have a cake?' Lucy smiled a real smile that lit up her heart-shaped face. 'Oh a croissant please and a milkshake.'

Chapter 28

It was Christmas day. Lucy woke at three, and lay in her bed with a smile on her face. She had just opened her stocking and the Father Christmas chocolates. Thank-you-letter notelets, colour pens and pencils and a rose quartz bracelet were neatly lined up on the floor where she could look at them. 'This is family life,' she thought, 'and I really like it. It feels so warm.' She thought about decorating the real tree that she had been allowed to choose, and how she'd put out a glass of sherry and a carrot for Father Christmas. She loved these rituals. 'I'm just like the other children now,' she thought. 'Oh, how I like not being different.'

Then she thought about Nick and her smile got bigger. How she had dreaded his coming, but now she felt differently about him. Right from the beginning he had been really kind to her, and he was fun, real fun. She thought back to a walk she had gone on with Nick and Benjy. They had both crunched through ice in a flooded field and the water had almost reached the top of her wellies. She remembered that conversation really clearly. 'Lucy,' he said, 'when I heard about you coming to live with Ma and Pa, I was really glad. I know Mum has always longed for a girl, and now you've answered that dream. I know how much she loves you.' 'Loves me?' said Lucy, widening her eyes. 'Yes, Lucy, loves you. You must have noticed how both Ronny and Jim care about you. That is love. They love having you in their home. This family would feel very lost without you.' 'You mean you too?' 'Of course, Lucy. I am really enjoying you. It might seem strange, but it's great for me, having a little sister. When I'm in Africa I think of you, and how happy you are making everyone.' 'What me!' 'Yes, Lucy, you.' He smiled, looking into her eyes. 'You do make people happy. You are so full of character. You've a real presence about you. It fills the house.' 'Don't you mind me being here?' 'Mind? No, of course not. I've just told you, you really add to this family. Because you are here, we're having a real family Christmas like we used to when I was your age. Besides, you're nearly as good as me at playing cards – especially 'Cheat, and Pelmanism.' 'Jim taught me,' smiled Lucy. 'You see,' went on Nick, 'without you all that would have stopped. Can't you see? Life is much more fun with you here.' Lucy did begin to see. Nick must have noticed her expression. 'Did you think I would spoil things for you Lucy?' She nodded, looking down so he wouldn't see her face. Nick lifted her chin. 'Look at me Lucy.' Look, I'm not jealous, just really glad you're here, my little sister.' Lucy smiled. She did believe him. His tanned face looked so sincere. Then she became aware that Benjy had run on to the next field. His nose, as always, pressed to the ground as he trailed rabbits. 'I'll go and get him,' she said, and ran on ahead, calling him as she went. 'I'm really wanted,' she thought. She felt buoyant and very warm inside.

Chapter 29

It was February. It was cold and grey every day and Lucy felt sad. Nick had returned to Africa and, like Ronny and Jim, she was really missing his large boisterous personality in the house. He had filled it, and the house felt quiet without his laughter. 'I miss my brother,' she told Cally at school, and Cally nodded with understanding. They had loved Nick. 'He's so handsome,' Daisy sighed.' 'I wish I had a big brother like that. You are lucky.' Lucy felt proud. It was such a new experience to feel lucky and to be part of a family that other people admired. Quite the opposite from what she had experienced with her mum. Then the other children had made horrible comments. The worst was being called dirty. 'You smell,' was one remark. 'You're just a dirty traveller.' Lucy found it almost too painful to remember. But now over a year later, nobody could call her names. She looked clean and well dressed, she was popular with her friends and they liked to come back to her house for visits and sleepovers. They even admired her. It felt so good. She thought about her mum often, usually with a guilty feeling, because she knew her mum wouldn't like her to be so happy away from her. She thought about this often. She knew she loved her mum, but she also recognised that she didn't miss the life she had spent with her. She never wanted to be cold, hungry and frightened again. She didn't want that feeling of insecurity, never knowing what was going to happen next. She never knew where they would be living, and who her mum would be living with. Some of her mum's friends had been friendly, but some had been horrid, drunk, woozy and wobbly, while existing somewhere else in their head. Her mum was always telling her, 'Don't worry, I'm going to get sorted.' It was always something out there that was going to happen but never happened. Lucy had spent all her life hoping it would happen, but now she was beginning to believe that it wasn't going to. That was so painful to accept. Then she would study Ronny and Jim. They were sorted. They did what they said and kept their promises. More than that, they not only wanted her to be happy, but they really put themselves out to ensure that she was. She thought about the jazz ballet lessons, and her hamster, and how she could have her friends over any time and how welcome she was in their homes too, because their parents trusted Ronny and Jim.

Sometimes she felt angry with them for being so reasonable and kind because it made her mum look hopeless, and more than anything she wanted her mum to be perfect. She tried to talk about it with Janet on one of their outings to Macdonalds: 'Sometimes they are so perfect,' she said about her new parents, I want to scream. I feel I want to bite and kick them because when they're nice they make my mum seem bad.' For once Janet seemed really in tune with what she was saying and listened without saying a word. 'I know it's not their fault,' Lucy went on. They can't help it; it's the way they are, but why can't Mum be like that too?' A huge lump filled her throat, and tears filled up her eyes. 'I always thought Mum would get sorted. If she loved me she would get sorted, wouldn't she? Wouldn't she?' Lucy repeated, really crying now. 'Why can't she be like other mums?' Janet spoke softly, after handing her a tissue. She was quietly relieved that Lucy was able to express her hurt. She knew that this was the start of any healing; the start of acceptance.

'Lucy, your mother does love you. She really does. Her not sorting her life is nothing to do with not loving you, though it must feel like that. It's just that she's chosen a way of life that different from most people. She doesn't mean to be a bad mother, but the life-style she leads is one that isn't often good for children.' Here Janet paused, trying to choose her words carefully. 'Sometimes people really don't know how to change their behaviour. The people around them are not good role models, so in some ways they don't know how to do it, or what they can do differently. You see, your mother deliberately chose her way of life because she wanted freedom. Now you have a role model with Jim and Veronica for a different sort of life. When you are older you can choose. You might be like your mum, or like Veronica and Jim, or somewhere in the middle.' 'I won't look after a baby like my mum did.' said Lucy fiercely. 'I won't want my baby to be different. I'll want it to grow up happy, like Nick. I want to do something for other children, like Nick in Africa, or work in an orphanage or be a teacher.'

Feeling so fiercely about it dried Lucy's tears. She could suddenly see she had a choice about how she was going to be. 'Ronny told me that we can choose what we want to be, and if we admire something, its good to see how they got to be like they are. I'm going to use Nick as my model. I'm going to make other children happy.' 'Well done Lucy,' said Janet proudly. 'And you will make lots of people happy, I'm sure of that!' Lucy grinned. 'Could I have an ice-cream?' she said. 'Of course, I'll have one too, and forget my diet.' Janet replied. Lucy and Janet smiled at each other. They both realised that a new understanding had built up between them.

Chapter 30

It was April and Janet was once again driving Lucy to Cornwall. This time it was going to be different. Her mum had finally received her prison sentence and was in prison for the next three months for shoplifting at the supermarket. Lucy could remember visiting her mum at a place like this before, when she was much smaller. 'At least she won't be with Dylan,' she thought. She had decided that Dyl was a bad influence on her mum. One good thing about having her mum in prison was that she knew where she was and that she was safe. She also had letters from her mum through Janet. Without much to do, Sarah, her mum, liked writing, Every letter was full of how, when she got out, they would be back together, and this time it would be different. Ronny had explained to her that she was under a care order for her protection, so this couldn't just happen. Her mum would first have to show that she really could look after Lucy properly and safely. This reassured her, as she dreaded returning to the life she had previously.

Ron had made her a very special box in which to keep all her letters, and Lucy also put Nick's letters and photos inside. He sent her lots of pictures of African children, which she had proudly taken to school to show the class. Ron had taken Lucy to choose the material for outside and inside the box. Then she had cut out the cardboard, put in padding and sewed the box together. Lucy had chosen pink checked gingham. She loved this box.

The way into the prison was grim. Janet and Lucy were taken through a side gate and along a long green-walled, green-linoed, corridor to a little room all painted beige, just like the Social Services one. Lucy thought the room had a horrible feeling and it smelt strange – stale cigarette smoke and disinfectant. It had a sign on the door, 'Family Room.' Here several comfy chairs with holes, where stuffing showed through, awaited them. 'I wonder who has picked at them?' she thought, 'Were they children visiting like me?' She and Janet sat in silence until the door opened, and Sarah was ushered in by a lady in a white shirt and navy skirt. She wore a tie like a school uniform. A fly buzzed, knocking against the window. There was a dead moth on the sill. 'Prisoners who couldn't escape,' she mused. The prison officer smiled at Lucy. 'Hello dear,' she said.

Sarah came in wearing blue prison trousers and a blue shirt. She threw her arms around her daughter. Lucy felt a bit stiff in her arms. It felt so unfamiliar. 'Lucy, Lucy, my baby, oh my baby!' cried Sarah, holding her daughter away to look into her face. 'Oh, Baby, so thin. You look so thin and pale,' 'No I don't,' thought Lucy, 'You know I look really well.' 'Oh, Baby, haven't you been eating? Have you been missing me? Oh Baby, I've been so unhappy without you.' 'Oh,' was all Lucy could reply. 'Why don't you sit down? said the warden. 'I'll be back later.' She and Janet left the room, but Lucy felt sure they were still outside. 'Oh, Baby, I've missed you. It's been so hard for me, you've no idea. It's so unfair. Aren't you sorry for your poor Mum, cooped up here, when it's spring?' 'Yes,' whispered Lucy obediently. 'She hasn't changed,' she was thinking. 'Oh, Mum, you haven't changed. You really don't understand what you've done. You just think life is unfair to you. Why can't you see!'

She sat there miserably while Sarah talked on and on. Why everything was unfair and how she had done nothing to deserve it. Lucy kept catching the word unfair, but her mind seemed to be in a blur. The door opened and orange squash and a plate of biscuits were brought in. Sarah took three biscuits. Lucy eyed the posters on the wall. They were all of summer holiday destinations. One showed a steam train, with someone waving goodbye gaily on the platform to a family waving through the window. 'A bit like my life,' she thought. She forced her attention back to her pretty mother who was still talking. 'Oh Lucy, it's been so hard for me, but you'll see! I promise I'm going to get sorted, and we'll be together, you'll see! Just you and me. We'll go to Cornwall and you can surf and we'll get a flat and we'll get a puppy.' 'Yes, Mum,' she said. 'I want to go home,' she thought.' 'I want to go home to my bedroom, and Ronny and Jim, and Benjy and Jessie hamster.'

Chapter 31

Lucy was very quiet when she got home. Jim and Ron seemed to understand. It was late and they tucked her lovingly into bed with a hot chocolate and a digestive biscuit. Lucy felt cold and very grey inside. She curled up in a ball, face to the wall, and clutched her teddy hot-water-bottle to her chest. 'She looks shocked,' Ronny whispered to Jim when they left her. I do hope she's all right.' 'Leave her be,' rumbled Jim, 'poor kid. She's got a lot on her mind; a lot of disappointed dreams I expect.' 'Oh, Jim,' sighed Ronny. 'Do you think she longs to leave us and go back to her mother? She didn't show any affection when she got back. It was as if we weren't there. Oh, Jim,' went on Veronica, 'I just couldn't bear it if Lucy wanted to leave us.' 'Don't fret, Ronny,' said Jim. Just let the poor child heal. She'll come round. Give her time.'

Lucy lay there in this strange, grey state. She felt frozen, numb inside. Memories of her mum running, bare-footed in the grass, her long fair hair floating behind her. Her mother's laughter when a butterfly sat on her hand. Her mother showing her birds' nests and ladybirds. Her mum giving her a chocolate bar for breakfast from behind her back, and a tub of pot noodles as a special treat. Her mother picking her flowers in the hedgerow and dancing around her, singing. Her mother taking her swimming in the river by a weir, and then drying themselves in the sun. Her mother singing her lullabies. All these, and more beautiful memories, floated past in her mind. Then others followed. She alone, in an empty caravan, too scared to cry, huddled under dirty blankets. The voice of one of her mum's boyfriends. 'Leave her, Sarah, let's go to the pub.' The terrible hunger and cold. Her mother making promises and then never keeping them. Being left alone all night. Lucy lay and mourned, too numb to cry. She didn't sleep till the early hours of morning. She knew now – Sarah wasn't going to change. Not for her anyway. Lucy felt terrible. Lucy felt totally alone.

Chapter 39

Lucy slept fitfully in the early hours of morning. She tossed and turned, and strange dreams kept waking her. Again she was all alone in an empty wasteland, and around her were slinking, snarling animals. Creeping low to the ground, hazy in the moonlight. She stood alone in the middle, while they circled around her, teeth bared. One looked like a fox, and one a bear. She woke at dawn bathed in sweat. Her head was pounding and she had a terrible pain on the right side of her ribs. It hurt to breathe. 'Am I dying?' she thought. She began to whimper, 'Mama, Mama!' She felt as if she was a tiny child of three. Her voice grew louder,' Mama, Mama!' Immediately the door opened, and someone leaned over her. 'Lucy, Lucy, are you all right?' She tried to open her eyes but her head hurt too much – she felt a cool hand stroke her forehead. Then, as if a great distance away, she heard the voice say, 'Quick! Ring the emergency doctors' number. She's burning up!' The voice sounded blurred as if coming from under water. Then she heard the same voice say, 'It's all right. I'm just going to sponge you with cool water. It's all right, darling.'

'Lucy screamed as the water touched her skin. It felt so cold against her flaming limbs. 'Pain.' She gasped, touching her ribs. 'Pain.' Tears squeezed from under her eyes. 'I'm floating away, it hurts.' 'I can't hold you Lucy,' the voice said, 'You're too hot, but the doctor's coming soon. You'll soon feel better.' Lucy drifted in the strange floating sensation. She couldn't move, it hurt too much. It hurt to breathe. Time meant nothing. She was vaguely aware of people around her, hands lifting her up on pillows, the bedding being moved from on top and cold air blowing onto her. She could hear someone groaning and realised it was herself. It hurt so much to be sat up that she screamed, and her eyes flew open. Then a new voice spoke: 'Lucy, this is Doctor White. I know it hurts but I need to listen to your chest.' She cried more. Then she was gently laid back against lots of pillows so that she sat up. She heard the voices more clearly now. 'It's Pleurisy,' the Doctor said. She felt something hard in her ear. Then the other side. 'Her temperature is very high,' She saw the man write something and give the other person a piece of paper. 'Can you get these antibiotics immediately? The other head nodded. 'And also give Calpol immediately. I'll give you something stronger for the pain. Keep her sitting up. I'll look in again at the end of the morning. She may need to go to hospital.' 'Mama, Mama,' whispered Lucy, 'Mama, where are you?' She was back in the wasteland. It was lit by moonlight and shadows flittered everywhere. Was that a wolf with yellow eyes? It came towards her. 'Mama!' she screamed.

Chapter 40

Lucy didn't need to go to hospital. By the next day the antibiotics were working, and Lucy had improved enough to stay at home. Her temperature had come down and she was no longer having those horrible dreams. She tried to tell Ronny about them. 'You were hallucinating,' Ron explained. 'That can happen with a high temperature and a chest infection. None of it is real, but how frightening for you!' Lucy nodded weakly. Her chest still hurt when she moved, and she had to be propped up all the time against pillows in an upright position. Her bottom felt sore from sitting on it for so long. Every time Ron walked her to the toilet she cried from the pain in her lung. Ronny and Jim took it in turns to sit with her, and she often held their hands. It felt very comforting. There were some yellow and blue flowers from the garden on her chest of drawers, and a tape recorder beside her so she could listen to her favourite story tapes. A lot of the time she slept. Her sleep had been so disturbed at night she was exhausted. Her face was still pinched and white, and she had dark circles under her eyes. She found herself crying for no reason. She felt very sad and limp. She thought about her childlike mother as she had seen her that week. She was so young and pretty, but she didn't understand how Lucy had needed her.
That evening she held on tightly to Jim's large reassuring hand and whispered, 'I wanted Mum, but she's never there for me' Tears began to run from behind her closed eyes. Jim squeezed her hand in his

warm one to show that he had heard. 'She only talks about herself.' Lucy's voice grew stronger. 'She steals things and gets into trouble, but she doesn't think it's her fault. She always thinks it's everyone else's fault. Why does she keep doing it? Why can't she be like other mums? Ronny is like other mums. Why can't she be like them too? I always wanted to be like other children at school. Now I am, but it's not with my mum. She's never there. She doesn't care!' She began to sob and Jim put his arms around her, and she was aware that Veronica had come into the room and had also put her arm along the top of her pillow. Lucy cried and cried. It made her head hurt. It hurt her ribs but she couldn't stop, and she felt glad they didn't try to stop her. 'Why?' she gasped, 'Why can't she be like other mums and be there for me? Why?' It hurt. The pain was inside her heart. And in her chest and head. She cried and cried. She wanted to scream and kick her legs, but the pleurisy stopped it. She just sobbed, and clutched at the bedclothes as she felt her grief. Her nose ran unchecked. She wanted to tear the sheets, to tear open her pyjamas. She was too weak, but it felt good to feel this. After about ten minutes the sobs got less, and she lay back on the high pillows totally exhausted. 'My head hurts,' she whimpered. 'I'll get you a cold flannel, darling,' Ronny said.

It felt wonderful, and so did the kind caring hand, smoothing her brown hair off her face – the hand that should have been her mother's. Lucy's voice croaked from the crying. 'I'll just give you your Calpol, darling,' Ronny's voice said. 'It's due now and it'll help the headache. It's only the crying that's given you the headache. You are getting better.' Lucy swallowed the medicine without any remonstration, and soon felt very sleepy. Holding Ronny's hand she drifted into sleep. A deep, dreamless sleep, that lasted for four hours.

Chapter 41

Lucy was in bed for a week. Sometimes she came downstairs, but tiredness would overtake her, and she would go back to bed, where she read her favourite books and dozed. She loved the story of Heidi because it had such a happy ending and she could really understand how Heidi had felt when she was so homesick in Frankfurt. She also loved the old video of 'The Sound of Music.' Both of these were totally un-cool and old fashioned, but they both touched on feelings that she knew. They were about people who didn't have proper parents, but they both had happy endings.

The pain in her ribs was still sore, but nothing like the original pain, and she could move around now. Ronny had spoken to the school and explained that she would be off for at least two more weeks. She had asked for a bit of homework that Lucy could do in bed. Lucy's teacher brought it herself after school, with homemade cards from her whole class, and a little posy of garden flowers from her teacher. This made Lucy feel very important and wanted. Cally and Daisy came to visit her too. Cally brought her two 'Animal Ark' books and Daisy had bought her a little Body Shop bag with shampoo and body lotion. Lucy was thrilled. 'I matter,' she thought happily. 'They miss me and they care.' Ronny and Jim spent hours sitting by her, and in the evenings she cuddled up on the sofa between them. Nick sent her texts. 'Hi, Sis,' I miss you. Get better quickly for me!' was the latest, and he also sent e-mails just for her – all about the children he was working with in the orphanage. Lucy found herself drawing and doodling in her sketch book she'd had for her birthday. She drew her mum, Dyl, Benjy, Jessie, Ronny, Jim, the garden, her mum's travelling van, Cornwall, everything. And on another piece of paper she wrote words in different colours, 'Anger.' 'Tears.' 'Pain.' 'Love.' 'Caring.' 'Fear.' 'Nightmares.' 'Friends.' 'Pretend.' She scribbled colours and shapes around them. It felt good inside to do this, and she began to talk to Jim first, and then to Ron, about how she felt. She couldn't stop. She told him about the nights of terror when she'd been alone, about the hunger, and her mum and all the broken promises, and how her mum never listened, could only talk about herself. She talked about the hurt. 'I used to beg so I could get something to eat,' she said. 'I'd look at the other girls in their lovely clean clothes and I'd long to be like them and now I am. I hated being dirty and smelly. I had to wash in old puddles sometimes and when it snowed I only had summer clothes and an old blanket.' She talked and talked, and cried, and felt rage, and a terrible sadness. Whenever she thought about Sarah, she had a pain in her heart, and it was hard to breathe. 'Why can't she love me, and be like other mothers?' she kept asking. Mostly Jim just squeezed her hand, and Ronny brushed her hair off her face. 'We are here for you, darling,' said Ronny, with tears in her eyes. 'I know,' said Lucy. 'I'm glad, but it makes it harder seeing mum isn't there. I so wanted Mum to be there. I so wanted it to all come right and that she would change and be like other mums, why isn't she?' Everyday Lucy talked about it. She even wrote a letter:

> Dear Mum,
> Why can't you love me like other mums do? Why couldn't you look after me properly? Why can't you listen to me? Why aren't you interested in my life?
> I love you loads.
> Lucy.

This time Sarah wrote back on pink paper, with Jemima Puddleduck in the corner:

> Lucy Babe,
> How could you write such an unkind letter to your Mummy. Those people are poisoning you against me. Of course I love you. I've always done everything for you. Do you remember when we'd go swimming everyday and I made you daisy chain jewellery for your hair, ankles and wrists? All the fun we used to have. Life is really hard for me Babe without you being so unkind. Dyl thinks it was all a set up, this prison thing. We are going to try Devon. Totnes is a really cool place. You can come to see us there. They have lovely food there. Remember how you loved brown rice and stir fries? We'll do that and go on the ferry to Dartmouth. We might see an otter.
> Your loving Mum.
> Sarah.

Lucy cried when she got the letter. 'It's like she doesn't hear me, or even know a little what I feel,' she sobbed. I want her to be my mum, and she wants me to be something I'm not as well.' 'Since I've lived with you, my life has been the sort of life that I've always wanted. I'm like the other children now, but you are like real parents but not my parents and' – she started to cry again. 'It's so confusing, I don't know what I mean!'

'We do, Lucy,' said Jim in his deep gentle voice. 'You make yourself very clear. What you feel about us not being your parents is so understandable. You want a magic wand to wave and everything will come right, but life isn't like that, sadly. But, Lucy, love is love wherever it comes from. Your mum loves you, but isn't able for whatever reason to take care of you properly, and we love you and love to take care of you, but we're not your mum and dad, but we love you living with us. We love you as if we were your parents and would be heartbroken if you left us, and so would Benjy, Jessie and of course, Nick, but if you wanted to leave us then we would have to accept your wishes. Lucy looked up into his outdoor tanned face with the crinkles round the eyes. 'Do you really love me?' He nodded, looking straight into her eyes. 'You didn't want your baby to die, did you? That wasn't what you wanted either.' 'That's right.' he nodded. 'But because she died it made you look for another girl, didn't it?' he nodded again. 'Yes, Lucy, and you came into our lives.' 'Like Annie in the musical?' she asked. He nodded again and grinned.

'Would you keep me for always?' Jim nodded, 'For always, of course we would.' 'And Ronny?' 'Oh, yes,' he smiled, 'Ronny loves you as our daughter. If you leave she will be very sad. But we do understand how you love Sarah just as you understand how we love Nick too. Love is very big, Lucy. It has room for many people. The more we love, the more we have. It's like that song.' Lucy grinned, hugely relieved.

'If you have a penny, give it away, and the more you have,' she sang. She suddenly threw her arms round Jim's neck. She felt so light inside suddenly as if a great weight had left her body. 'I think we'd better call Ronny, don't you?' Jim smiled. 'It's time for a celebration. What shall we have?' 'Elderberry cordial and chocolate biscuits and then a walk with Benjy,' she commanded. 'Elderberry cordial it is then,' chortled Jim. Lucy felt she could talk to Jim more easily, as she sensed Ronny might be hurt. Jim understood this. 'Ronny is the sort of mother who puts her children before everything else, their growth is paramount to her. I think, Lucy, when you grow up you may be like that too.' 'Oh I will,' said Lucy with heartfelt feeling. 'Oh I will.'

Chapter 42

In the months that followed Lucy felt very happy. The time of her illness had changed something deep within her. She no longer felt as if her life was temporary. She felt as if she was where she belonged with Ronny and Jim. Her friends accepted her and her family unquestionably, as if it was all as normal as their own lives. Occasionally a brief card came from Sarah, who was back with Dyl and travelling around Devon: 'Looking for our Nirvana!' she had written. 'I feel we are so nearly there!' After finding out the meaning of Nirvana, Lucy decided that perhaps she had found hers first.

In the summer, they were again on holiday in St. Ives. It was beautiful weather, and the previous evening they had all been on a boat trip and spotted dolphins. Lucy was ecstatic. She suddenly realised this dream of seeing dolphins had come true. It hadn't been with her mother but with Ronny and Jim, and she realised it no longer mattered who she was experiencing it with. She knew she was in the right place with the right people, and her life was exactly as it should be. She was eleven years old and just about to go to Secondary School. She had two loving parents, a beautiful Mum looking for her Nirvana, and wonderful friends. She, Daisy and Cally were moving on to the next school together so wouldn't be separated. She stood in front of her parents, water dripping, body-board clutched to her, and said – 'Ron, Jim, would you ever think of adopting me so I

could really belong?' She didn't need an answer. Both their faces
 broke out in smiles of incredulous delight. Then the three of them were locked in a great hug of love.

Printed in the United Kingdom by
Lightning Source UK Ltd., Milton Keynes
137536UK00002B/59/P